Ash Bear

(Daughters of Beasts, Book 3)

T. S. JOYCE

Ash Bear

ISBN: 9781797405896
Copyright © 2018, T. S. Joyce
First electronic publication: November 2018

T. S. Joyce
www. tsjoyce.com

NOTE FROM THE AUTHOR:

Published in the United States of America

First digital publication: November 2018
First print publication: November 2018

Editing: Corinne DeMaagd
Cover Photography: Wander Aguiar
Cover Model: Jonny James

DEDICATION

For the beautiful badasses.
(that's you.)

ACKNOWLEDGMENTS

I couldn't write these books without some amazing people behind me. A huge thanks to Corinne DeMaagd, for helping me to polish my books, and for being an amazing and supportive friend. Looking back on our journey here, it makes me smile so big. You are an incredible teammate, C!

Thanks to Jonny James, the cover model for this book. I love getting to work with him. And thank you to Wander Aguiar and his amazing team for this shot for the cover. You always get the perfect image for what I'm needing.

And last but never least, thank you, awesome reader. You have done more for me and my stories than I can even explain on this teeny page. You found my books, and ran with them, and every share, review, and comment makes release days so incredibly special to me.

1010 is magic and so are you.

ONE

Love meant something different to everyone.

For some, it was freedom.

For some, it was pain.

For some, it was a distraction.

For some, happiness.

For some, it was home.

But for Ashlynn Kane, love had been utterly...unattainable.

Love was for smart girls who read a lot, who could talk easy and flirt. It was for the outgoing girls who knew how to curl their hair into perfect beach waves, contour their cheekbones, and make everyone in a room laugh.

Love was for girls who were everything she was

not.

Mousey, quiet, shy, slow to speak because the words in her mind didn't come out right when she opened her lips... Who could be a match for that?

Her father, Bash Kane, had always told her there was a mate for everyone, but she was twenty-eight years old and had never even had a serious boyfriend.

One of her dear friends, Remington Novak, bumped her shoulder gently and said, "Look, she's here." Remi pointed to the front door of Sammy's Bar, and the blaring country music faded away.

Her other best friend, Juno Beck, walked through the crowd and froze, stared at her mate up on stage with her lips slightly parted. She looked so different than the last time Ash had seen her. She wore her hair down and was in ripped-up black jeans and a black tank top that hugged her curves instead of those stuffy pant suits she wore when she was schmoozing her music clients. But how she dressed wasn't the only change. Juno didn't look tired anymore, and her cheeks were rosy. She looked so pretty.

A huge smile stretched Ash's face as she arched

her gaze to Rhett Copeland, Juno's mate, playing a concert up on stage.

Remi leaned back and rested her cheek against Ash's, and Ash put her arms around her and hugged her neck. Remi sighed. She was a good friend, happy for Juno, just like Ash was happy for her.

"Holy shit, y'all, she's here," Rhett said from the stage.

The crowd erupted in cheering. Remi did one of those shrill whistles, but Ash was more of a clap softly and watch kinda girl.

"Damn, you're a sight for sore eyes, woman," Rhett said into the microphone. "I fuckin' missed you."

"Awwwwwwwww!" came the chorus of girls.

"Booooo," called a man with a mohawk a couple seats down the bar.

"Yeah, boooo and barf," Remi's mate, Kamp, called out, cupping his hands around his mouth.

Remi was laughing really hard.

"I have the worst friends in the world," Rhett said with a chuckle.

He was talking to the crowd, but Ash was already in her head again. He'd called Remi a friend, but Remi was *her* friend. And Juno's. She didn't know these people—these Rogue Pride shifters. And Remi and Juno were different now, so vibrant and alive while she was exactly the same as she'd always been. Same old Ash. Everything was confusing. Everybody had left her and changed and come back, but she didn't fit anymore, did she?

Brighton and Denison Beck were making their way to the stage to sing with Rhett. He was staring at Juno like she was the most beautiful woman he'd ever seen.

Someday, she wished all of her 1010 wishes would come true and a man would look at her the way Rhett looked at Juno.

"Your hair is puffy," growled the man a few seats down the bar.

He probably wasn't talking to her so she let herself get lost in the ooey, gooey, lovey eyes Juno and Rhett were making when he said into the microphone, "This one's called 'Goodish Intentions.'"

"Awww," Ash murmured low, snuggling her cheek against Remi's. This was the song Juno's dad had written for her mom. She'd always loved it, and now her mate was singing it to her.

She'd also made lots of 1010 wishes that her friends would find their mates, and at least those had come true.

"I said your hair is puffy."

Ash frowned at the man leaning on the bar top with both elbows, his hands clasped around a glass of beer. His black hair was styled into a mohawk, and his neck was covered in tattoos. He wore a gray thermal sweater with the sleeves pushed up, exposing tattooed forearms. His gold eyes were extra squinty as he glared at her.

She had wished someone would look at her like Rhett looked at Juno, but all she got was an insult and a tattooed behemoth staring at her with his golden eyes all angry-looking.

"Me?" Ash asked, patting her hair with one hand.

Remi narrowed her eyes at the giant and said, "Suck a tit, Grim."

"And blue," he said, his voice all snarly and low.

Ash stopped petting her blue hair and ducked her gaze. This man—this Grim—was very dominant. He filled the whole room with that icky feeling of being too big for his skin. He felt like the dragons did when they were here, which...one of them was. Damon

Daye, the Blue Dragon himself and owner of the mountains she called home, was sitting at the very end of the bar, frowning at Grim.

Monsters. Too many monsters.

And when she glanced up to check, the monster with the mohawk was still staring at her.

"I don't hate puffy blue hair." Grim ripped his eerie yellow gaze away from her and went back to staring at the television that was playing an infomercial for some gadget that took the shells off of boiled eggs. The volume wasn't even on, and everyone else in the room was watching Rhett Copeland sweeping Juno off her feet.

He really didn't seem to care at all, just sipping his beer every thirty seconds or so. Not that she was paying attention, but she was good at counting. She didn't have smarts about other stuff, but she could count good and she was good at computers like her dad. So far those little party tricks had earned her zero attention from the less-fairer sex.

This was usually the part where she clammed up and didn't respond or look at a person for the rest of the night, but she was feeling brave because, look at Juno and her bright smile, and look at Remi leaning against Kamp as he whispered into her ear. This Grim would go home to his mountains soon, and she would never see him again. He wasn't like all the other shifters here who lived in Damon's Mountains and knew how she was. He was different, a stranger. Mom had always told her strangers were bad, but to Ash, they were good. Sometimes she could be braver with strangers.

Layla was working the bar tonight, and right as Ash opened her mouth to say something to the gargantuan tattooed man, Layla interrupted with a, "Here you go, Ash." And then she slid her a shot of tequila and a lime. It was her favorite drink because, for some reason, it reminded her of tacos, and she loved tacos. "Thank you," Ash said as she pulled the shot glass closer.

Layla gave her a knowing nod and then twitched her head at the giant. "Go on then."

Ash's hands started shaking. This was a bad idea. The music was so good, but it was loud. The stuff that made sense in her head never came out right. That man had something bad inside of him. Something very very good, but also something very very bad. She'd seen men at war with each other, but never a man at war with himself, but she felt more stuff than other shifters felt, and Grim was a mess-up like her. A glitch. He was different from other shifters, and that almost made her brave enough to talk to him, but then maybe she should just take this shot and be quiet. Like always.

So she did.

She took the shot and sucked on the lime to calm the burn in her mouth, and then she pushed the shot glass toward Layla to convince herself to pay attention to Rhett and Juno. But then the Grim man, without even looking away from the television, said, "I'll buy that one for her, and can you get her another?" He lowered his scary gaze to Layla and finished it with a low, rumbling, "Please."

Layla's arms were resting on the counter, and when he looked at her, she froze. All the hairs on Layla's arms lifted as if she'd touched an electric fence.

But Grim had offered to buy Ash a drink. So that was nice. Something good and something bad in him. Something good and bad.

"Sure," Layla said softly, and then Kong was there. Her mate. Big-ass silverback gorilla shifter the size of a tank with a shaved head, staring at Grim from the other side of the bar. Monsters. Sooooo many monsters. Ash's hands shook and shook.

Grim blinked slowly and glanced at Kong, didn't look impressed, and then went back to watching the infomercials.

Ash craned her neck to look at him because Remi and Kamp were making out now and were in the way. "Um. Thanks. Thank you."

The man, Grim, didn't answer.

Ash couldn't find it in herself to say anything more until Layla gave her the second shot. Awkwardly, ever awkwardly, Ash lifted the glass in a silent cheers to him, tapped the bottom of the bar top to ward off angry spirits like Beaston had taught her to do, and then she drank it fast. And when she opened her eyes from shooting that throat-searing booze, he was watching her again. Eerie yellow eyes taking in everything.

"S-s-something..." She dropped her gaze and quit.

"Something is wrong with you," he said.

Frowning, she forced herself to look at him when she said, "I was going to say that about you."

"I know." He turned to the TV. "I was guessing

what you were thinking. I figured that's what you were going to say about me. It's what everyone says."

"Oh." She spun her shot glass slowly on the bar top. "You didn't mean that about me?"

"Nope. There's nothing wrong with you."

Ha! "Wrong." *You're wrong. Say it like "you're wrong."* But the words wouldn't come out.

Grim inhaled deeply, looking annoyed. Everyone did that around her—looked annoyed. Not Juno and Remi, though. Ever since they were cubs, they'd taken her under their wings and stuck up for her.

"Move," Grim snarled at Remi as he stood.

Remi shoved him hard in the shoulder. "Fucking make me, prick."

A snarl ripped from him, and he leaned within inches of her face. Remi laughed and said, "Just kidding. I just like to make you mad." And then she smiled sweetly as she switched to the next bar stool. "But if you hurt her feelings, I'll kill you, then Change into a bear and piss on your body and set it on fire and let the ravens pick your bones clean."

Ash leaned forward and enlightened her with, "Ravens wouldn't want to eat a body that tastes like bear piddle and kerosene."

Grim snorted and took the seat beside Ash. He dipped his attention to her hands, which she was wringing. She pulled them into her lap and dropped her gaze. Sometimes she hated being submissive.

"Blue hair, black at the roots, but your eyes are blue like your hair. They look bright. Little nose and curves that could give a man something to hold onto when he fucks her. Quiet. Which is surprising since you've done your make-up and hair with confidence, but you keep looking at the bar top. That's not something wrong, though. It tells me your submissive. Right or wrong?"

"Right," she breathed.

"You wore a tank top in the dead of winter. You don't get cold."

"Bear."

"Mmm," he murmured, nodding. Approval? He hadn't asked her animal. That part had just slipped out.

"You're fine. Me?" he said, arching one dark eyebrow. "I'm not, but I would never say something is wrong with you. That's like the pot calling the kettle black."

She didn't understand. "Kettles *are* black."

"So are souls."

"Not yours. Not all of it," she rushed out on a breath. "You have good and bad."

Now Grim was frowning. She couldn't hold his gaze. Couldn't. He felt too big. Too scary, too exciting, but too scary. But so exciting.

Her heart was pounding like a drum.

Grim glanced at the neck of her tank top and back up. A slow, crooked smile took his lips. "I hear that racing heart. Don't be prey, pretty blue-haired lady. The bad in me likes it too much."

"Should...should I go?"

"Nope. Just relax. Enjoy the music and sit by a strange stranger for an evening. No one will hurt you here."

From down the bar top, Kamp griped loudly, "I can't even fuckin' believe you've had an entire conversation with her, and you haven't said a word to me in three days."

"Well, you're a fuckface, and she isn't," Grim muttered, staring at the television once more.

Well...that was sort of a nice compliment. Kamp was a fuckface, but she wasn't. Huh. She liked that.

The tequila shots were kicking in, and everything

felt hazy. "Hair school."

Grim took a long drink of his beer and then turned to her. "That's where they did the blue?"

She nodded. "I got it done at the hair school because it's only fifteen dollars for a cut and color and blowout on Tuesdays."

"Do you want to be a cosmetologist?"

Wow, he knew what that was. But she was messing this up. *Take your time to say it right.* "I do hair and make-up just for myself. I serve barbecue. For money. For work." She cleared her throat and took a deep, steadying breath. "I mean barbecue is my job. Not hair."

Grim's eyebrows shot up like he was impressed. She giggled with relief. That was her move. When she did something good, she laughed. "Last Tuesday, the students at the hair school were working on bright colors. So I figured, why not? It's not my favorite, though."

"Why not?"

"Blue is my least favorite color. It's like skies on a hot day, but I like it when it's stormy. Not because I'm sad. I mean, I like cloudy days."

"Your hands are shaking."

"Talking is…" She looked at her phone but it was 11:11, not 10:10. She made wishes on 10:10 not 11:11, but she still poked her finger on her phone screen and made a wish that he could understand her. "I'm no good at talking."

"But you work in barbecue. There must be talking involved."

She shrugged up one shoulder. "I'm strange. Too. Also."

Grim lifted his chin higher and looked down his nose at her. He was much taller and was very thick with lots of muscle. His eyes had softened to a light brown, and he had a big beard. He was young, maybe her age, but his eyes looked like they had seen a hundred years. His skin was pale white, but covered in black tattoos. He was the most striking and handsome and terrifying man she'd ever seen.

There was this loaded moment when he looked at her lips, and she thought he might kiss her, but instead, he dropped his attention to her empty shot glass. "Do you want something else?"

Oh. He was one of those boys. The ones Juno and Remi warned her about. The ones who wanted to get girls drunk and take them home. Disappointment swirled in her chest.

Grim turned to Layla who was walking by behind the bar and slid a five-dollar bill and a credit card across the counter. "Can I get her an ice water, close out my tab, and get some quarters?"

"You got it," Layla said, taking his cash and card.

Okay. He wasn't trying to be one of those boys. He was getting her water. Okay.

Grim asked, "Do you like games?"

"Head games? No, I'm no good."

Grim chuckled. "I'm not good at head games either. I mean pool." He angled his head and got a thoughtful look on his face. Or maybe a confused one. She wasn't good at reading faces. He thanked Layla when she brought him a receipt to sign and a stack of quarters. To Ash, he asked, "Do you want to play pool?"

"Yes," she whispered fast. But the guilt kicked in. "I'm no good."

"You keep saying that, but I have this feeling you're very good."

"Oh," she said, heat firing her cheeks as she shook her head. "Wrong."

"I don't mean at pool. I think you are good in

general, aren't you?"

Ash shrugged. "I donate blood on Fridays."

He had a nice smile. It was slow, like he didn't give them easy, and she liked when he gave them to her. A person had to probably earn smiles from a man like him. A man who had good and bad.

She stood and followed him as he made his way to the pool tables in the back.

Bad was okay.

As long as the good in him was bigger.

TWO

Truth be told, he'd asked the shy, curvy, blue-haired beauty to play pool because the pool tables were in back, away from the audience crowded around the bar and stage. She'd seemed so uncomfortable, that his instincts to fuck everyone up had become a little overwhelming. He would need to Change tonight and give the Reaper his body.

Like he had control of that. Ha!

He needed her to settle down so his inner lions would settle down with her. That had been his intention, but when she'd talked, she'd interested him. He couldn't figure her out. She was shy, and she spoke differently than anyone he'd met before. He liked it, though. She was different from all the viper females of his old Tarian Pride.

Grim racked the balls without looking at her. People reacted better when his focus wasn't on them. Even humans. Even puny, weak humans had some long-buried instinct that they were in danger around him. Sometimes it helped if he didn't look at them, but with this girl, it was hard not to. He'd never seen anyone like her.

She had sky blue hair that was down to her shoulders and black at the roots. Her eyes were bright as the sky, and even though blue wasn't her favorite color, it was his. Everyone else in this bar looked exactly the same—except her. It was as if a light was shining brighter on just her, casting everyone else in shadows. She was an impossible woman not to pay attention to.

Big tits, big hips, and she had that hourglass figure that he'd always wished for in a mate, if he'd been allowed to take one. Her tank top flattered her curves and showed the top of her cleavage, and he couldn't deny his attraction to her. But he also liked the way she felt. It was like a stream of goodness was seeping into his skin from her. Did she realize she was like that? That she could feed the dark ones like him or the dragon shifter at the end of the bar who was still paying him too much attention? Ash was a feeder. And he was an eater. An eater of the good, and he would drain something pretty and sweet like her.

It was a good thing the Rogue Pride Crew was leaving tomorrow because Grim would pay this girl way too much attention.

"What's your name?"

"Ash. Ashlynn. But just Ash. My dad picked it. He's Bash. I'm his first daughter, and he likes words that rhyme." She wrung her hands in front of her lap and said, "Oooh." Her cheeks turned bright red.

"You're doing good," Grim said as he rolled a pool stick on the table to make sure it wasn't a shitty, wobbly one. It was about as decent as an abused bar-pool-stick could get, so he handed it to Ash. Ash. Pretty name for a pretty woman.

Her skin was smooth and pale, like some ice princess. Even more so with those bright baby blues and blue hair. She was a stunner, and it was hard to look away. "Do you have any tattoos?" he asked.

"No, but I like yours."

Grim smiled. He couldn't help himself. He didn't often get compliments. Something dark and sickening roiled inside of him, but he ignored it. That was just the Reaper waking up. He would want the body soon, but Grim was used to it. There were plenty of big predator shifters here to keep him from killing anyone. Probably.

His good lion faded away like he did every night. Typical weak move. He rarely took the body. He always gave in to the Reaper.

"Your name is Grim. Does it rhyme with your dad?"

He grinned and gestured for her to break. "No dad, no mom, no rhymes. Grim isn't my real name. It's just what everyone calls me."

"You don't have a family?" she asked as she slammed the cue stick into the white ball and broke up the balls at the other end of the table.

Huh. Well done.

Ash loosened up when he wasn't focused on her, so he chalked up his pool stick and didn't look at her when he said, "I was raised by my grandmother. Her name is Rose. No rhyming."

"Roses are pretty," she uttered softly.

That they were. "I grow them in front of my trailer for her." Holy fuck, what had possessed him to say that out loud? Grim cleared his throat, lined up, and hit the two ball in. And then the one. He missed on the six, though, just so she would play with him longer.

"We used to have roses," Ash said, lining up a shot. "Clinton pulled them all up and threw them on the roof of our trailer. Twice. Now, no more roses." She talked so much easier when she was busy.

"What color roses?" he asked.

"Pink."

Grim hid his satisfied smile. "That's my grandma's favorite color. I cut the thorns off and mail them too her every two weeks during the growing season. Her mate used to get them for her, but he died before I was born. And I was the man of the house, so I always got her pink roses so she would know...how...special..."

"She's very special," Ash said with wide eyes and a curt chin nod. "I like her."

Good God, he'd just poured his fuckin' heart out to this girl. He'd never told anyone that.

Did he like this? Was it okay? He didn't know. Maybe that beer was stronger than he thought.

The Bartender, Layla, showed her knack for

perfect timing and brought a pitcher of ice water and two glasses to the table next to the pool table. Grim poured them both glasses. *Time to sober up and stop talking, motherfucker.*

The Reaper growled.

Fuck you.

The Reaper growled louder, rattling around in his head. Grim closed his eyes tightly for a three-count until the monster eased away and then brought Ash one of the waters.

"Does it hurt?" she asked softly.

"Does what hurt?"

"The Good and The Bad?"

Grim didn't understand, so he handed her the water and took his turn at the table. Another two balls in and a purposeful miss on the third.

"Mine hurts," she said quietly as she lined up for another shot. She sank the eleven in the corner pocket. "And I only have The Good."

Grim narrowed his eyes at her. "Who told you?"

"That you have two?"

"Yeah. Who told you I have two animals? Was it Remi?"

"Oh, Remi is loyal to Rogue Pride. She barely says

anything. It hurts sometimes that she doesn't talk to me like she used to. It's supposed to be like this, though. She's supposed to pick her Crew. It's supposed to hurt. It means she's doing it right."

Grim leaned against the wall, gripping his cue stick as he crossed his arms over his chest. He really didn't understand, but before he could ask, Ash shrugged up her shoulder and said, "No one had to tell me. I can feel The Good and The Bad in you."

Huh. This girl was hella interesting. "And you aren't scared of The Bad?"

"I haven't seen him. How can you be scared of something you can't see?" She looked at him with such wide-eyed innocence that, for a moment, he wished he was a normal shifter with one animal. One who had a shot at staying stable. One who had a shot at not disappointing everyone. At disappointing her. If she saw "The Bad" she would run away and never come back.

He hadn't named the Reaper. He hadn't named the dark lion. The Tarian Pride had. A Pride full of monstrous, murderous lions had named the two most important parts of him—Grim and Reaper—and he was standing here looking at this good girl, wishing he was a little less dark so he could talk to her longer.

But it wasn't the way of the world. Not for him.

Grim leaned over, lined up the shot, and scratched on the eight ball. "You win," he murmured. "It was nice to meet you, Ash."

"Where will you go?"

"Now?" he asked, setting his cue stick in the rack in the corner.

"Yes."

"Now I'll go where The Bad tells me to."

And then he forced himself not to look back as he made his way down the hallway toward a back exit. Because he knew exactly what he was giving up. He was giving up an evening with a nice girl who could make him feel a little bit normal. But the Reaper didn't care about such things, and there were woods out back.

The Bad was a-scratchin', and it wasn't his choice to answer the door or not.

The Reaper did what he wanted.

THREE

Grim was almost as wide as the hallway. Shifters tended to be bigger, especially the males but, holy crap, Grim was bigger than Kong. He walked like an Alpha. Felt like one, too. Was he the Rogue Pride Crew Alpha? She needed to ask Remi more questions about her new Crew.

Ash had done something wrong, she could tell, because he was leaving so fast. He'd barely lost the game of pool, and now he was running out the back door.

She should find out what she did wrong so she could learn and be better.

So...Ash followed him.

She followed him down the hallway and out the

back door, catching it as it swung closed on her. She followed him down the narrow back stairs and past the blue dumpster. She followed him into the packed parking lot and past the clusters of Rhett Copeland fans, all here to hear his music from outside of the packed Sammy's Bar. She followed Grim straight into the woods and walked and walked until he stopped, far away from everything.

That gray thermal sweater showed the lines of his muscular back. He was tensed up and breathing heavy. "Why are you following me?" he asked in a voice that sounded like it was more animal growl than human tone.

"So you won't be alone," she answered.

"It's not safe to be around me."

Ash looked back toward the bar, but they were too far away for her to even see the lights. "Not safe for a bear or for humans? There is a difference, Grim, whose real name is not Grim. Humans bleed easy. I do not."

"What do you want from me, Ash? Say it quick so I can get you to go away."

Ash shrugged. She was a shrugger. She shrugged, then went and sat down by a tree and rested her back against the rough trunk. "To be near you. So you won't be alone."

Grim cast her a golden-eyed frown over his massive shoulder. "How could I ever be alone if I have two animals inside of me and a Crew inside that bar?"

"The animals aren't your friends and neither is your Crew. You didn't ask them to come out here with you," she pointed out.

"I hunted them last week." He turned slowly and stalked closer. "I set up a drinking game in the woods, and I listened for them to get closer and closer." His voice had gone low and feral. "And then I tried to kill them."

Ash picked up a stick and broke it in half, then drew a circle in the snow so she could give her attention anywhere but his scary eyes. "I killed a lady bug last Thursday. It was an accident. It was on my jeans, and I scratched my leg. Killed it with my bare hands. I also ate pizza three times last week, and now my jeans don't fit. We all feel guilty. Stop hunting them."

"That's just it, Good Girl." He knelt down in front of her, and she could hear it so clear—the growl in his throat. He hooked a finger under her chin and

29

lifted her face to his. "I don't want to stop hunting them." He snarled up a lip, and she could see it. She could see him losing himself. Ash wasn't talking to the same man who had been nice to her in the bar, and it made her angry. It made her want to yell at the imposter who was trying to intimidate her.

His eyes flashed a chocolate brown for a moment. He gritted his teeth, angled his face away. Sweat broke out on his forehead.

"Can you hold it?" she asked.

"It's not like taking a piss, Ash." Whooo, that voice wasn't human at all anymore.

"I know a place if you can hold it."

When he looked back at her, his eyes were gold again. "I want to rampage."

"But we could rampage together, away from all these humans, and then sit in the hot springs after we're all done."

Grim's dark eyebrows drew down. "What's the hot springs?"

"Big-ass hot tub. Hold it like piss, Grim. And then we can have more fun."

For a moment, he knelt there in front of her with wide eyes, lookin' at her like she was crazy, but that was okay. Everyone did that when she opened her mouth. She was used to it.

He had pretty eyes when they were all wild and gold like this. The moon was full, and she had good vision on account of the bear that lived inside her, so she could make out even the little green specks in the middle. His black mohawk was all spiked up, and his beard was thick but trimmed. He had really nice lips. The kissable kind. At least, she thought so. She hadn't kissed that many people.

She'd never been into tattoos, but Grim's were like artwork on a canvas. She shouldn't say it, but if she didn't, she might never get the chance to. So...she inhaled deep, closed her eyes, and rushed out, "You're pretty."

"Ash..." Grim's voice broke on her name.

And when she opened her eyes again, his face was red and he was shaking. His closed fists were punched against the ground, and every vein in his forearms and neck was popping out.

"The Bad?" she whispered, fear flooding her.

"Run," he barely got out before his body broke into something monstrous.

A lion with paws the size of her head and a pitch-black mane ripped out of him and landed with his legs splayed on either side of her hips. His lips were curled back, exposing long, razor-sharp teeth, and his gold eyes were full of more hate than she'd ever encountered in her life. There were no green specks in his eyes anymore. Only fire-yellow.

His breathing was ragged as he leaned closer, closer, until his forehead pressed against hers. and then he pushed her back into the tree behind her. This was a terrible position to be in, sitting, un-Changed, under a monster with his weapons ready. Teeth and claws and anger. *Be ready, Bear.* Her voice shook as she asked, "Grim?"

The lion tensed, eased back, lifted an enormous paw with his claws extended, and then time slowed. Something deafening rattled the woods, a roar she hadn't heard in years. The moon was blotted out as a massive creature covered the sky, beating its wings as it landed behind Grim, crushing the trees under its talons.

Grim turned, a snarl in his throat as he faced the Red Dragon. Vyr Daye. Vyr was home in Damon's Mountains. Fully Changed into his fire-red dragon and narrowing those icy blue, reptilian eyes at Grim as he lowered his horned face low enough to the ground that his dragon-smoke breath blew across the woods like fog.

And The Bad...that deranged animal with too much dominance in one body and no control... charged Vyr. He charged a dragon twenty times his size.

"No!" she screamed, and Vyr reared back. She scrambled to her feet, but it was too hard to see. There was too much smoke, and the lion had disappeared into it.

She could hear it—the terrifying sound of Vyr's Firestarter clicking in his throat.

And then there was fire.

It lit up the fog, illuminating the lion's silhouette as he skidded to a stop just in front of the line of inferno the dragon had made.

Fourteen seconds. She counted them in a whisper to calm herself down. She was real good at counting. Counting came naturally. Fourteen seconds Grim The Bad stood at the fringe of the fire, looking up at the Red Dragon. Fourteen seconds, and then he turned and disappeared into the woods. He didn't look back. She waited to see if he would.

Vyr watched him go, his scaly nostrils flaring with each infuriated breath, and then he glanced at Ash, swiped his massive claw through the flames, extinguishing them, and dug a smoking trench in the earth as he did. And then he bunched his muscles, lifted his great horned face to the sky, and beat his wings. The wind was so strong she plugged her ears and stabilized herself against the trunk of the tree until he was gone.

What...the hell...had just happened?

Pressing her sweating palms to her cheeks, she looked where Grim had disappeared into the woods. She lifted her attention to the sky where Vyr was just a speck in the distance, then back to where Grim had disappeared again. She didn't understand.

She'd never seen Vyr as a dragon. From rumors, he'd been a beast when he had Changed in Damon's Mountains when he was younger. But Vyr was very different now. He'd found a mate. He'd been lucky. He'd found a crew with Nox and Torren, but now he was back? For what? To blow fire at Grim but not kill him?

She didn't understand anything.

Part of her was angry at that. She never

understood why people did what they did. Nothing made sense but numbers.

"Was that a dragon?" a human asked from a few trees away. He was swaying and had a beer bottle in his hand. Probably wandered out here to take a leak and got lost.

Huffing a frozen breath, Ash stood and gathered Grim's boots, wallet and cell phone from the back pocket of his tattered jeans. His clothes were ruined, but she could keep the other stuff safe. She marched toward the drunken human and stopped right before she passed. "Fourteen seconds he had to kill the lion, and he didn't."

The man arched his eyebrows. "Okaaay."

"I don't get it either. Better get back to the concert, human. It smells like smoke out here."

FOUR

When Ash saw green eyes reflecting in her headlights, she slammed on the brakes of her Jeep and skidded to a stop inches away from the black-maned, scarred-up lion in the road. She'd come barreling around the curve, just like every night, because she was the only one who lived out this way. Never having to worry about other cars on the one-lane wilderness road, she had always set her own speed limit.

Grim was so massive, he would've totaled her Jeep if she'd run into him. He still could if he had a mind to get inside of it, but he backed away from the headlights, and she could see it. His eyes were green, not gold. Just pure, bright green, like rain-bloated moss. *Hello, The Good.*

Grim hunched in on himself and groaned in pain as he Changed back to his big, muscular, tattooed human form. Looked so painful she couldn't rip her gaze off him if she tried. He was letting her see it, so she should be brave enough to stay in it with him. Sometimes she didn't like Changing alone either.

On hands and knees, Grim shivered in the road, his head down as though ashamed. He wouldn't look at her.

She should pull around him and speed away. That's what smart girls would do, but she wasn't one of the smart ones.

"Are you sick?" she asked as she shoved open the door.

With a soft grunt of pain, Grim rocked back and rested on his bent legs, rolling his head backward so he looked down his nose at her. His skin from neck to shoulder was badly burned.

"Ooooh no," she murmured, echoing his position and kneeling down with him.

When she reached out and touched his neck lightly, he winced, but his eyes never left hers. They were muddying to a brown color instead of green. Brown and green and gold. Grim had problems.

"Would The Bad have hurt me?"

"The Reaper," he rumbled. "His name's the Reaper. And I don't know. I don't have much control over that one."

"But the green-eyed good one?"

Grim frowned. "What do you mean?"

"The lion with the green eyes. The Green-Eyed Good."

His frown deepened, causing wrinkles on his forehead. "You saw green in my eyes?"

She nodded once and tugged at his arm so she could see how far back around his neck the burn went. "Stupid lion. Whatcha gonna do? Kill the Red Dragon?" She shoved him in his good shoulder. "Don't do that anymore."

Grim's breath was steady as he studied her. Her attention dipped to his thighs. Or more specifically to his long, thick dick. She tried to stop looking but couldn't.

"It happens every time I Change," he murmured, looking down at himself.

"What does?"

ASH BEAR

"I get hard. I don't freaking know why. Changing doesn't exactly feel good. It's the adrenaline maybe."

"It's…"

"It's what?" he asked. He was so direct when he asked questions, it made her want to answer instead of chickening out.

"It's real pretty."

"My dick is pretty?"

She clasped her hands tightly in her lap. "If you're looking for a girl with good words…that's not me."

"You talk clear enough to me. Okay. My dick is pretty." When he shrugged, she smiled.

"I'm a shrugger, too." She pulled her shoulders up to her ears to demonstrate.

He shrugged.

And then she shrugged faster.

And then they both started wiggling their shoulders double time and she couldn't keep a straight face anymore. She cracked up.

And there it was, that stunning smile of his. It was right at the very corner of the left side of his lips. It made his face go all crooked. She liked crooked things. And Grim? He was a very crooked type of thing.

"The hot springs are far away from here," she said apologetically. "They would help the burns, though."

"I'll be healed by morning," he assured her. Huh. Tough man. Dominance sometimes made a shifter heal even faster. He must be very dominant.

"Are you the Alpha? Of Rogue Pride? Of Remi and Juno?"

"Not on purpose." He stood and held out a hand to her.

She looked at it and then him. Brown eyes. Pretty human brown eyes. She slipped her palm against his and allowed him to pull her up. He was very strong. She was surprised how easy he did. She wasn't some teeny girl. "Why are you here?"

Grim took a couple steps back and rested his hands on his hips, stared off into the woods, then shook his head. "I don't know. I just...wanted to come here."

"You mean the Green-Eyed Good did. He wanted to come here."

"Smells like you," he murmured. "The whole forest smells like you. Like your bear."

Ash wrung her hands nervously. "You smell my bear?"

"Yes. She's...she smells pretty." Crooked smile, there it was, and now there was a spark of life in his eyes to match.

Ash giggled and kicked at a clump of snow with the toe of her shoe. "No one's ever said that before."

"Well..." Grim looked around. "Okay. I should go."

"Go where?"

"Back to the bar. All my damn clothes are back there. And my Crew. And my cell phone. I need to figure out when we're leaving in the morning."

"Oh. Well I saved your boots and wallet and cell phone. They're in my Jeep. But if you want to go back to the bar, it's ten miles thataway." She pointed down the mountain helpfully. "Your pretty dick'll freeze off, though, if you hike it."

"I'll be all right," he murmured with such confidence that she utterly believed he would be just fine. Strong man.

"I made meat?"

Grim turned and cupped himself. His skin was looking paler, and he had gooseflesh. He must've been very cold out here. "What?"

"I have food I made last night. It's nothin' five star. Pot roast and mashed potatoes and gravy and carrots and stuff."

Grim shifted his weight. "Well, hell, that sounds five star enough for me."

"I can share. With you."

Grim scratched his jaw and studied her with a canted head, as if she was some sort of bug that needed figuring out. It was a quiet few seconds before he murmured, "I won't Change again tonight. The Reaper is sleeping now. I can take a couch or the floor or something. I swear I won't come onto you."

"Well, that's a little tragic. It's okay if you don't want to come onto me. Everything's okay," she said, making her way to the Jeep. "I got heated seats so your ass doesn't freeze."

"You mean so I don't freeze my ass off?" he asked.

Ash giggled. That was the saying. She'd forgotten it. He made good jokes.

When he got into the passenger's seat, he admitted, "I don't want to see my Crew again tonight." His voice was so quiet.

"Why?"

He rested his elbow on the edge of the window and stared out if it, away from her, biting his thumbnail. He wouldn't answer, but that was okay.

Sometimes she didn't like to talk either, so she put the Jeep in gear.

But then he spoke up. "I don't like the Reaper. I don't like that part of me. I don't really like being around people after I'm him." Grim looked over at her, but she didn't understand what he was trying to say with his pretty eyes.

"Why?" she asked again.

"Because I'm ashamed." He reached forward and turned up the radio dial, and that was that. Conversation over. He was ashamed of the Reaper, and she bet he hadn't admitted that to many people.

That made her feel special, and she wanted him to feel special, too, so she gave him a present. She reached over, rested her hand on his thigh, and squeezed it gently. Shifters loved touch. It was a comfort. It was her way of saying, 'It's okay with me that you are how you are,' without her messing it up with actual words.

He didn't even tense up, just sat there staring at her hand on his bare leg. She left it there as she drove with her free hand until she reached the little cabin she rented from her landlord, Mr. Perkins.

"You aren't scared of me," he rumbled as she

opened her door.

"Well, you feel very big, and part of you is scary, but the other part is nice. Plus, Vyr looked like he wanted to burn you and eat your ashes tonight when the Reaper came out. He'll probably avenge me if you kill me."

Grim huffed a surprised-sounding laugh. "Yeah, he burned the Reaper right out of me."

But she didn't understand what that meant so she said, "You can get out, and we can go inside and eat. Or eat out here if you like the wild. Sometimes I like eating in the wild."

"What do you mean in the wild?"

"Outside. A picnic." She got out and closed the door behind her, then crunched her way through the snow to the little cabin she'd called home for three years.

"That actually sounds nice. I just don't have any...you know..."

Ash turned around to see what was wrong, and he was standing barefoot in the snow, boots in one hand, and the other hand still covering his man-bits.

"Oh! Clothes! Don't worry. I have an idea for that."

FIVE

A bull.

Grim cocked an eyebrow at himself in the full-length mirror in the spare bedroom. Ash had handed him a Halloween costume in the form of a thick adult onesie that had hooves on the feet, a fuzzy belly, and a hood with horns.

It barely fit him and was tight in the dick area. The sleeves were too short, and he couldn't get it zipped up past his belly button, but it was warm. So...there was that.

He would've cursed Rhett for begging him to come to Damon's Mountains except he actually didn't mind tonight. Ash sure did have his interest.

And...well...bull onesie and all, he was kind of...sort of...having fun.

He made his way out of the bedroom into the living room. God, this place smelled so good. Ash was in the small kitchen heating up the food, and he couldn't remember a single time in his life anything smelled better.

The best part of it all? When he saw Ash, she was wearing a black and white spotted cow onesie, complete with horns and udders.

She turned around with the brightest, prettiest, most genuine smile he'd ever seen on another person. Like she was really happy to see him.

"Moo." Ash giggled as she clutched a bowl of mashed potatoes in her hand. Her nose scrunched up with her laugh, and the psychotic part of him wanted to touch it just to feel the cute little wrinkles there.

Biting back a smile, he murmured low, "Moooo."

Now Ash was cracking up, her blue hair falling out of the cow hood in little wavy wisps as she moved. He wanted to touch that, too.

"I thought if I dressed up, too, you would be happier."

"It worked. You look..." *Beautiful.* He cleared his

throat. *Careful now, Grim. She isn't yours.* "You look like a cow." *Shit. That was rude, and not at all what he meant.*

But Ash didn't seem to mind him calling her a cow. She just stifled her giggles and said, "Me and Remi wore these a long time ago to a Halloween party, and Juno was a bucket of milk."

Okay, now he was really having to fight a smile because he could just imagine the three of them. "Here, let me help." He took the potatoes from her and piled spoonful's onto the two ceramic plates she'd set out. She'd already dished up pot roast and carrots and some type of bread cut in a triangle.

When he pointed to it, she said, "Yorkshire pudding. My mom makes it better."

Well, then, her momma must've been a chef or something because it looked and smelled delicious.

"Do you like to cook?" Grim asked.

"I like to cook when I'm confused."

"What do you mean?" he asked, searching the cupboard for glasses so he could make them drinks.

"Beer," she murmured, pointing to the fridge.

Even better.

"I get confused when people are mean, or

sometimes when they are nice, and cooking helps me think about it."

"It's your therapy."

Ash shrugged up a shoulder. She hadn't zipped up her cow costume all the way, and she had a tight little tank top underneath where he could see her cleavage. When she looked up at him, her clear blue eyes looked so bright, and her dark eyelashes touched her cheeks when she blinked. He'd never thought a blink could be sexy before but, holy shit, she was so fuckin' beautiful. Total showstopper.

If he was the old Grim, the enforcer Grim, the Grim that was in charge of fighting for the Tarian Pride, he would've dragged her rank near the top no matter how submissive she was. He would've brought her closer to him and burned anyone who said a single thing against it. He would've started a war in the Pride for Ash. And that right there was one of the many reasons he wasn't at the top of the ranks in the Tarian Pride anymore. Dominants bred with dominants, and submissives were treated like shit. But he didn't think like the others. He didn't believe only dominants should be important. Good God, he didn't even like dominants. What had the Reaper ever done for him? Made his entire life a nightmare, that's what.

Grim reached for the handle to the fridge and winced as the movement tugged on the burn across his neck and shoulder. It was bad. He was healing, but the material of the onesie was rubbing on it and irritating it worse.

"Here," Ash said, yanking open the freezer. She pulled out a package of frozen peas and slid it through the opening of his costume. He tensed a little at the shock of the cold, but after a few seconds, he sighed in relief as the burning eased.

When her phone dinged on the counter, she frowned at it but ignored the glowing screen and went back to heating up one of the plates. It dinged again.

It was two a.m., so when the third notification lit up her screen, Grim gave into his curiosity. "Is it Juno and Remi?" he asked innocently.

"No, much worse."

He frowned. Something long buried inside of him didn't like that. He wanted to snuff out whatever made her pretty, dark eyebrows frown and that full bottom lip pout.

"Are you okay?"

"I am on a match site."

"A match site," he repeated.

She shrugged up her shoulders. "To find a mate."

Nope, did not like that at all. Zero stars, did not fuckin' recommend. He nearly choked on his snarl. "You deserve better than a blind-date mate."

"I don't deserve anything," she said lightly. "Here." She handed him a plate and picked up her own. "Wild dinner?"

"Uh, you mean do I want to eat outside?"

"Yes." She nodded. "That's what I mean."

She was changing the subject, but she was about to learn something about him. He was a relentless hunter. "Yes, dinner outside sounds good." He grabbed a blanket off the back of the couch as he passed because something inside of him wanted to protect her from the wind. And he had a feeling that something had green eyes and didn't see the light of day much. The Good, as Ash called his steady lion, was pushing the Reaper to the edges. He could feel a little war going on inside of him for headspace. Both lions were watching her, The Good with interest, The Bad as prey. Ash wasn't safe with half of him.

Grim hated himself.

She led him down the porch stairs to a fire pit out in the yard with a couple of white plastic lounge chairs. Her sexy ass swayed left and right, her little black and white spotted heifer tail pulling another smile from a face that hadn't smiled in a while. She didn't even realize how fuckin' cute she was.

She set her plate down and picked up a lighter off a stump table by her chair, but Grim stopped her. "Go on, sit down. I'll tuck you in and start the fire. Eat before it gets cold."

Ash froze like a sexy little moocow popsicle. Her cheeks turned the same pretty pink of the roses his grandma loved. So pretty.

The Reaper growled.

Fuck off, Reaper. Let me have one night with someone who makes me feel okay.

"Th-thank you," she murmured as she relaxed onto the chair with her food in her lap. She lifted the plate for him to put the blanket over her legs, and then she watched him pull logs off a low pile next to the iron ring fire pit. The peas almost fell out of his costume, so he had to zip it up better before he could light the crackling, dry newspaper underneath the logs.

"You look pretty again." She whispered it so softly he almost missed it over the growling in his throat. Fuckin' Reaper was going to make him miss her weird compliments.

"What's the match site you're on?"

Ash was taking a sip of her beer and sputtered and coughed. Recovering quickly, she said, "It's silly."

"It's just me and you here. We can say whatever we want."

"But..."

"But what?"

"I want to keep you. For tonight."

She was worried he would leave? "You have me. For tonight." He wanted her for longer, but he was going to leave her alone and let her have a good life. Not poison her with the Reaper.

"There's a site that got started a long time ago in Damon's Mountains. 'S called bangaboarlander dot com."

Grim purposefully kept his face as composed as he could. "Okay." He adjusted the burning logs with a rusted iron poker he found on the ground. "I can't imagine you needing help to find a mate."

Ash kept her gaze on her plate as she moved her food around with the tip of her fork. She went quiet, and he could almost, almost smell some emotion coming from her—sadness?

He sat on the chair next to hers and took a long swig of his beer, studying her, waiting for her to talk to him.

When she didn't, he finally pushed. "You okay?"

"I don't like being teased."

"Who teased you?"

"You're doing it. I know it's a joke, you saying I shouldn't have trouble finding a mate. I don't like it."

Aw crap, he didn't mean to make her feel like he was making fun of her. "Look at me," he murmured.

When she shook her head, she looked so sad it punched him in the gut. Fuck. He wasn't good with people. He hurt everyone. This is why he was king of the Last Chance Crew.

He should leave. He should get up, set his plate down, walk into the woods, and never come back. The Reaper inside of him gave a slow smile. He couldn't stop snarling. He wanted to hurt the thing that had hurt her, but that was him. He was the hurter. Always the hurter.

For once in his life, he wanted to give smiles instead. For her. Feeling like shit on the bottom of a boot, Grim pulled his chair right next to hers and gently gripped her chin, bringing her gaze to his. "I wasn't teasing. You have pretty eyes and a figure that makes my balls clench just walking behind you. You have a sweet disposition, and you care about people. You don't just waltz through your life unaffected by the people around you. You're a good friend to Juno and Remi, and you think a lot about other people's feelings, and—"

"I ain't one of those smart girls. And my body is shaped like a number eight, not a number one. I live here alone and will probably never leave the Boarlanders. No boy has ever stuck around because I don't make sense to anybody, and nobody makes sense to me. I've been on bangaboarlander for three years since Juno set up my account for my twenty-fifth birthday, and people always message, but they don't care about me after I respond. I bore them."

Grim released her chin because, truth be told, he felt like he'd just stuck a fork in a light socket. "None of that matches the girl I see. And besides, eight is my favorite number. You're the least boring person I've ever talked to. Fuck anyone who made you feel that way. Give me a list, and I'll take care of them."

"W-what?"

"A list, Ash. Give me a list of those boys' names who made feel that way about yourself. Fuck anyone who ever made you feel like you don't make sense." He gritted his teeth so hard his jaw ached. "You're just about the only thing that's made sense to me in years."

SIX

Ash sat there stunned. She made sense to him? A trill of excitement zinged through her that made her want to make him presents. Pizza rolls and pocket knives and heart-shaped cards and all the special stuff she'd watched her friends in Damon's Mountains give their mates over the years. She wanted to make more smiles on his face. Pretty smiles, not the ones like when he gritted his teeth at his Crewmates at the bar.

"How did you meet your people?" she asked, suddenly desperate to know more about him.

"You want confessions? It's probably best to get them out of the way, and then you can decide whether I sleep inside or outside tonight."

She shook her head slightly. What did that mean?

Grim pushed the bull hoodie off his head, adjusted the peas on his shoulder, relaxed back against the back of the lounge chair, and stared at the fire. "I'm in Rogue Pride to exist until I get too tired to keep going."

Those last two words broke her heart. "Don't say that. Don't be tired."

He gave her a small crooked smile that didn't reach his amber-colored eyes. He growled a lot. Between sentences, between words, even when he was just sitting there. "I was raised in the Tarian Pride. They made me who I am. Made the Reaper. I was born with a dominant lion, raised with the intention I would Challenge for Alpha someday. I was brought up to hate everyone. My grandma was a submissive lioness. Both my parents were killed in Pride politics when I was a cub. There was a council, five dominant lions who chose kings for the Pride. They'd chosen me when I showed I liked to fight early on. So when I wasn't with my grandma, they were training me to be a killer. It's all I knew. I had my grandma trying her best to keep me good, but I had the council reinforcing the bad. Started fighting when I was twelve. I wanted to fight everything. To kill every male who even looked at me wrong, and the council was proud of that. I was rewarded for every fight won. And then I lost a fight. A big one. I was eighteen. There was one other lion being brought up to be high in the ranks. An asshole named Justin Moore. Justin was a problem. He was a womanizer. He thought females were there for him to breed when he took Alpha and nothing else. They existed to give him future cubs. They were nothing more than a wet hole to stick his dick in. Made me sick, watching him treat the females like shit. We hated each other. *Hated.* If a male ever treated my grandma the way Justin treated the females, I would kill him slow and not lose a second of sleep. We had to homeschool because the council was creating monsters who couldn't be in a public setting. So, we were kept nestled in the heart of the Pride, built like weapons, taught the politics, taught how to work the Pride, taught how to be ruthless Tarian kings, knowing one of us would rule the Pride when the Alpha got too old and weak to hold it. One of us was born to kill him."

Grim looked over at Ash, his eyes sparking with

something she didn't understand. "Do you want to run yet?"

But he wasn't evil. Just tortured. Her eyes burned with tears because she wished for a better story for him. She wished he'd had an easy time growing up. She pushed the hood off her head, set down her plate, and threw the blanket around her shoulders like a cape. Then she crawled onto his lounger right behind him and wrapped the blanket around them both. She hugged him up tight because that's what her dad had always taught her. If someone was broken, a hug could keep their pieces together.

"Keep going," she whispered.

Grim inhaled deeply. "I've never talked about this before. Not out loud. I've only replayed it in my head."

"Tell it to me like a movie. Take me there. Tell me about how the Reaper came to be."

"Okay." Grim sucked in a deep breath and patted her hands on his stomach. "I lost a fight to Justin. We nearly murdered each other, our lions hated each other so bad. We both ended up in the middle of a field, in the middle of a bad storm, bleeding out while the Tarian Pride stood around us waiting to see which one of us died first so our families could be honored or stripped of their honor. You like stormy weather, but rainclouds always remind me of the day I died. I remember my grandma screaming and crying as the council held her back. She wanted to help me, but I couldn't be helped. I was built to die or survive in that field. I tried to hold on. I wanted to keep my eyes open so bad, but everything hurt, and my lungs weren't working right. I was so cold. I tried to focus on my grandma. Her hair was down, silver already from stressing over the monster I turned out to be. It was whipping in the storm. Tears were streaming down her face, and her eyes were bright green like my lion's used to be. She Changed and fought everyone, but there were too many, and I lost sight of her in the mass of lions. I couldn't move. My fuckin' neck was ripped open. I was lying there painting the grass red. I died first."

"Oh my God, Grim."

"I didn't see God when I died. I saw something much worse."

"What?" she asked, but she was pretty sure she knew the answer.

"The Reaper. I woke up in a basement with a blanket over my body. Something was burning inside of me, something awful and dark. There was an incinerator going, heating up a dank room. That was the hell I'd been meant for, but hell was being born inside of me instead. I Changed over and over and over, just...body buckling in on itself. It was a glitch or something. My old body was still fighting, but the Reaper wanted complete control, so he took the body and gave it back and took the body and gave it back, just playing with it like a bored cat with an injured mouse. Every second that went by felt like an eternity, and I begged for the council to kill me. Anytime I heard them talking outside the door, I begged. Begged and begged and begged. Begged until my voice wouldn't work anymore. I was an eighteen-year-old kid in more pain than anyone could imagine. I Changed like that for three days. Didn't eat, didn't sleep, just Changed until my body didn't feel pain anymore. Until I was numb, lying there on that burial blanket, staring at a wall, dead enough. The council didn't know what it meant. I felt so different to them, and I was. The lion inside of me that would've made a good Alpha for the Pride was almost snuffed out of existence. He was barely there, while the Reaper...well...he was the new king. Justin lived, and my rank couldn't be recovered after a loss that bad, so the council came up with a new job for me."

Ash wrapped her arms around him tighter. "What was it?"

"Enforcer. I was the bullet whenever the Tarian Pride went to war, had a territory dispute, or had a scuffle with a rogue, anything. I was the killer, and the Reaper loved it. He grew stronger and stronger until he destroyed all the good parts of me."

"No," Ash murmured. "Not all of them."

Grim frowned and angled his face to the side. Mohawk, tattoos, so many scars.

She rested her cheek on his back. Pretty monster. "I'm not a smart girl, but I can feel good parts of a person. You don't go by the Reaper because you are still Grim. I saw green eyes tonight. You're still here. The Reaper just had to exist keep you alive. You gotta angel and a devil in you, Grim Reaper. That devil ain't won yet. I don't want you to be tired. I want you to stay."

"In Damon's Mountains?"

"No, I know your story isn't meant for here. I mean, I want you to stay on this earth. If you exist, everything can be okay."

Grim rubbed his hand over and over her clenched ones squeezing his stomach. He stared into the woods. "You really think so?"

"Well, you said I make sense. And I never did that for anyone before. I like that feeling. You'll go home to your mountains, and I'll be here in mine, but my heart can be happy if I know that somewhere out there you're okay." Ash kissed his tensed back gently. "If you're okay, that means I'm okay, too. Grim?"

"Hmm?" he rumbled.

"I want to be your friend."

"I can't be friends, Ash. I'll hurt you."

"I accept."

"What?"

"I accept that you'll hurt me. But try not to, okay?"

There were a few loaded moments when she just sat there, hugging him tight to make sure all his pretty pieces stayed together. The clearing was silent, the wind was still, and the only thing she could hear or feel was the pounding of Grim's heartbeat against his sternum, against her hand.

"I'll try."

And that's the most she could ask for from a broken man—effort.

He was too smart and too good for her, but she was going to make sure he was safe, no matter what. Reaper or Grim, she didn't care. She just wanted the good parts of him to keep going and keep fighting. She would be a proud friend and a secret cheerleader for the Alpha of Rogue Pride.

SEVEN

Kill her.

Grim sat up in a rush and nearly fell off the edge of Ash's guest bed. It was dark as pitch. Not even moonlight filtered through the open window. Must've been covered by clouds. A memory of him lying in that field washed through his mind. He really hated clouds. He could feel the cold breeze on his skin. Always, always he had to sleep with the window open, no matter how cold it was. The Reaper needed fresh air. That part he understood. It was left over from the days in the basement in the dark, the birthplace of the Reaper. He couldn't go back to feeling trapped.

Kill her, the Reaper whispered again.

Those words were so clear, the Reaper could've been sitting right beside him instead of in his mind. It used to give him chills, but he'd accepted the demon in him a long time ago.

Grim scrubbed his hands over his face. His skin was clammy, and he was uncomfortable from the inside out, but couldn't decide if he was too cold or too hot.

Kill her.

"Shut the fuck up," he murmured, but something curious happened. The same words were whispered softly in his mind at the same time. *Shut the fuck up, Reaper.*

Grim stumbled from the bed, his legs tangling in the bed sheets. He nearly went down, but caught himself on the edge of the mattress and then scrambled for the light switch. He flipped it on as soon as he could and looked around the room.

He was alone.

Kill her.

Shut the fuck up...Reaper... The old whisper rang with familiarity as it faded to nothing on Reaper's name.

Couldn't be.

Couldn't.

Be.

Was that the old lion? The one he'd been born with? The one that had been stifled by the bad in him? It had been so long since he'd heard him, Grim couldn't be certain. Maybe he was just going crazy as usual.

"Hello?" he murmured, desperate to prod The Good, as Ash had called him, to the surface of his mind again. But there was nothing there. Not anymore.

Kill her.

"Shut the fuck up, Reaper," he gritted out again. This time it was only his voice.

His body pulsed with a sick, dark power. He shook his head and fought the nausea that threatened to double him over. Grim didn't want to Change again. He wanted to keep Ash safe, and he couldn't do that if he was The Reaper.

Kill her.

"Why?" he demanded through clenched teeth, gripping his hair, pulling it as his stomach churned and his skin tingled.

Because we don't understand her. She's different. Submissive. She makes me feel...

"Makes you feel what?" he choked out. The Reaper never talked, never seemed confused like this, and Grim had to know.

She makes me feel. I don't like it. Make her stop. Kill her.

Grim groaned and stumbled out the door. His movements were jerky and forced as he made his way along the dim hallway, backlit by the bedroom light behind him. *No, no, no. Reaper, stop!*

He watched his hand push open the door. It creaked softly, and inside, Ash was laying on her bed, facing him. Her eyes were trained right on him, and she didn't look surprised.

"The Bad is loud."

Grim swallowed hard, but it felt like a lump of cement moving down his throat. "Ash?" He didn't know what he wanted to say. *Run? Help? Fucking use your magic and fix me?*

"Come here," she murmured.

"I shouldn't, Ash. I'm not okay."

Yes, the Reaper whispered. *Go to her.*

Creepy motherfucker.

Ash sat up in bed and pulled the covers back to make room for him. Didn't she realize this was a bad idea? Didn't her instincts scream that something was wrong? Couldn't she sense the Reaper? Grim was nearly choking on him.

Chest heaving with shallow pants, he made his way to her. She was wearing a short purple nightdress with a V at the neck. The hem was riding up her thighs. Her legs looked so smooth and pale in the dim light coming from behind him. He bet if he touched them, they would feel like silk.

Carefully, he sat on the edge of the bed.

Ash shocked him to his bones by cupping his cheeks. "I see you."

Grim frowned. "What do you mean?" Fuck, his voice was so scratchy. He sounded like a monster.

"You were talking to yourself. Your gold eyes— they're pretty like the sun, but hard to look at like the sun." She flipped her hand over and dragged the back of her knuckles down his beard. Felt so good, he almost, *almost*, purred. The fire in him was dimming, but the Reaper was still here watching her.

"My real name is Joshua." He didn't know why he'd told her that. He hadn't uttered his given name since the Reaper had been born. It felt strange just to form the word. "I guess I just wanted you to know."

She looked at him, looked at his bare chest, at him, at his bare chest. Submissive, pretty girl, he couldn't blame her. Most people had trouble holding his gaze.

"You're not bad, you know," she whispered. "You're different, but different doesn't mean bad."

Why was his heart pounding so hard right now?

Her hands on his face felt like heaven in a bottle. Like four shots of whiskey after a hard day. Like before the Reaper, before his life got so fucked up, before the Tarian Pride made him what he was. Maybe it was Ash who was The Good.

He leaned forward and kissed her. He didn't know what possessed him to do that; she was better off living her whole life without a touch from him. He couldn't even blame it on the Reaper taking his body. This was all him. A growl rattled up his throat, but he ignored it and so did Ash. She tasted good. He wanted more, but he also didn't want to fuck this up, so he eased back. She just sat there, her little chin lifted high, her lips puckered, her eyes closed, her cheeks turning redder and redder. And then there was this tiny smile on her lips that did something to his insides...something good. The snarl died in his throat.

Pretty girl.

Sweet girl.

Smart girl.

Sensitive girl.

Understanding girl.

A man searched his whole life for a ride or die, but it was impossible to know what that looked like until you saw it in a woman's essence, her personality, her reactions. Ash was special. More special than she realized.

She opened her eyes slowly, and they were glowing an icy blue color, several shades lighter than they'd been before. There was her bear. Fuck, she was a stunner.

"You aren't wearing any pants."

Grim snorted in surprise and looked down at his raging boner. "Nooo, I am not."

She glanced down at his dick, and her smile got brighter. "That's big. It's like the size of my arm."

Okay, now he was chuckling. "That's an exaggeration, but my ego thanks you."

"Well, I don't know how to flirt, or even seduce a

man, so if you ever want more from me, you will have to say a code word or something."

Grim leaned back on the bed and stared at the ceiling fan. "Like what?"

"Like...let's diddle." She giggled and plopped on the bed right beside him. "I like talking to you. It's easy."

He shook his head in mock shock. "Woman, you're the only one in the whole would who would say that about me."

"Well...if I say something wrong, I will just remind you that you're crazy and I will get a free pass."

"Ha! Probably."

"Your insanity is like a safety net."

He grinned over at her. She was loosening up and talking easier. Atta girl.

"I wish you didn't have to go back," she said suddenly, resting her cheek on her arm and plucking at a loose thread on the bedspread. "I like having you around."

"I've only been around for a few hours," he reminded her.

Ash shrugged up her shoulders. "Feels like

longer."

And she was right. He'd just met her at the bar tonight, but he'd already told her his real name and admitted things he'd never said out loud to anyone. There was something here. Something big. He wanted to keep her.

Kill her.

The Reaper's whisper was a punch to his stomach. Ash was a hummingbird, and he could never protect something so fragile from himself. The Reaper would pluck off her wings just to watch her hurt. He couldn't allow that. Grim would die before he broke this sweet bear.

He reached over and brushed a blue strand of hair from her cheek and away from her glowing eyes. And then he gave her another admission—the biggest one yet.

"You'll be better off when I'm gone."

EIGHT

Grim was hot.

Ash crossed her legs and leaned back against the pallets in the back of Moosey's Bait and BBQ. It was break time, which meant staring-at-a-picture-of-Grim time.

She'd totally snuck a picture of him early this morning, out in the freezing cold, his bull onesie covering the bottom half of him, the top half unzipped and hanging off his muscly butt like it didn't want to let go and, damn it all, she didn't blame the costume. She'd never been jealous of fabric before, but she supposed there was a first time for everything.

The picture was him standing over the chopping block, ax raised in the air, six-pack flexed as he prepared to slam the blade into a log. His tattoos looked extra dark against his chilled, pale skin. And his arms were thick like tree trunks. She'd never felt like a small girl before, but around him, she felt like the size of a fire ant.

Just gonna zoom in a little...

Oh God, right where the zipper was opened, she could just make out a light happy trail. Why hadn't he wanted more than a kiss last night? He was hard and she was wet, and they would've been good together. But he'd been content to just fall asleep beside her on top of the covers.

When she'd dropped him off at the hotel this morning, she'd gotten real sad because she had to say goodbye to him. The Rogue Pride Crew would all fly back to Oregon today, and her life would go back to being boring.

Her phone lit up with a message from the bangaboarlander site, but she did what she always did and swiped the notification banner up to make it disappear. She had better things to do, like stare at Grim's rib muscles. Was that a real thing? Rib muscles? He looked like he had rib muscles.

Another message popped up from the site, and Ash glared at it. How dare whoever this was interrupt her Grim ogling?

In a huff, she opened it up to tell him *thank you but no thank you, there will be no romance found here*, but the user's name was Joshua.

Ash's eyes bugged out of her face and she nearly choked on her gum as she stood up in a rush. She opened the message.

I like your bio. It was very...enlightening.
Joshua

She didn't even remember what her bio said. Juno had set it up years ago, so Ash exited the message and went to her profile page. It was an old picture of her with plain black hair like her dad's. She was looking off to the side with a flustered smile on her face. She remembered when Juno took that picture. It was a big holiday party for all of Damon's Mountains, and there were so many people there it had been uncomfortable for Ash. Everyone talked so fast sometimes, it was hard to keep up with their conversations. It was easiest if she was quiet and laughed when other people laughed. She hadn't talked hardly at all that night. But her sweater was kind of pretty. Maybe that's why Juno picked that picture to post. For her purple sweater. Purple was the color of grapes, and grapes were Ash's very favorite snack.

"Ash!" Audrey called from inside. "Break's over."

Crap. Ash speed-read her bio, which was actually her reading super slow because she wasn't very good at it.

I'm one of the good ones. Sweet, passionate, non-judgmental, double-D boobs, always up for a good time, soft-spoken. Pro-shifter interest only. Humans are okay. Must want a family. Must be good with animals. Must not be a douchebag. I work at Moosey's BBQ therefore I'm every man's dream. I can pour a beer with very little froth on top, and I always smell like meat.

Ash scrunched up her face and sniffed her shoulder. Did she?

Hobbies include: skinny-dipping…

What the heck?

Cooking the best damn food this side of the Mississippi, boning, and taking sexy lingerie pictures. I have great feet for those of you with fetishes. Likes butt stuff.

Dear God, had someone changed her profile? She didn't remember any of this!

Also, this profile update is brought to you thanks to Juno Beck, because Ash is very good at hacking airline apps and almost got me fired. Payback is a biyotch.

There were two middle finger emojis and a gif of a girl twirling her wrist and taking a bow.

Ash's bear growled. No wonder she was getting all these weird messages lately.

"Ash!" Audrey called.

All she wanted to do was stand in the freezer to cool her fiery cheeks and change this profile back to something not ridiculous, but Audrey, the mate of Ash's Alpha, Harrison, took that moment to throw open the door. "Girl, you need to get in here. You have customers waiting."

"What? But...Brandt is working still, isn't he?"

Audrey was wearing a weird smile. "Best you get to the front counter quick."

"O-okay." Ash followed her boss past the

refrigerator, down the hall, through the indoor barbecue pits, to her register.

And who should be standing there but Grim himself, wearing a tight black T-shirt, a blue and black flannel shirt, a gray beanie, and a bright smile that stopped Ash dead in her tracks. "Grim?"

The smile reached his eyes and made them crinkle at the corners. Pretty, pretty man. Her heart was trying to jump out of her throat, so she swallowed really hard to keep it inside of her.

"Hi," she said, making her way to the register. She looked around to find Juno and Remi ordering food from Brandt at the register down the counter, but mostly they were staring at Grim with matching frowns and squinty eyes.

"You look pretty," he murmured, his face turned away from his Crew, his eyes locked on Ash.

"Y-you also do that. Look pretty, I mean." She huffed a breath because her lungs felt funny. Wringing her hands didn't help, so she picked up a stack of paper menus and busied herself with straightening them. "I thought you had to go," she murmured.

"Rhett decided to stay a few more days to record

in the Beck Brother's studio over at Sammy's Bar. He told me to leave, but I think I'll stick around. You know, to piss him off."

"Oh. Oh, yes, pissing him off would be good."

"Plus...I wanted to see you again."

"Me?" she asked too loud.

Grim chuckled and cast a quick glance at his Crew. "You're fun to be around."

"I'm a great friend." Heck yeah, she was going to sell herself! She wanted him to stay, too!

"Yeah, but fortunately her friend card is full," Remi griped. "Stop looking at her like that, Grim. She's not a steak."

"Well, if she was, she would be a porterhouse," Rhett said nonchalantly from where he was standing next to Juno, popping open a bag of Cheetos.

Juno elbowed her mate.

"Ow! What?" he asked, glaring at whatever look Juno was giving him.

The country crooner looked from his mate to Ash and back. "She's grown. She can get whatever dick she wants to. If she wants to slum it with Grim, who are we to tell her no?"

"Rhett!" Remi yelled.

He hunched his shoulders at the shrillness. "Are you seriously being a cock blocker? Remington Novak, you've been bitching for three months about how Grim needs to get laid, and now you're cock blocking him?"

"Laid by anyone other than my best friend!"

"There's no laying," Ash whispered, mortified.

"And furthermore," Juno said, "Grim is a damn monster. Ash is innocent."

"No, no, no, no," Ash murmured a little louder, pressing her cold palms to her heated cheeks.

Grim snarled. "Says the girl who put that she likes butt stuff on Ash's profile."

"Don't growl at her, man," Rhett said, anger flashing in his eyes.

Oh no, they were definitely going to fight.

"Can we get through one fucking meal without a brawl?" Kamp asked from where he was pulling a beer bottle from a bin of ice.

"No!" Juno and Remi said in unison.

"I'm not innocent." Ash's cheeks were on fire. It felt like someone had doused her in kerosene and lit a dang match on her face. "I'm not," she reiterated to Grim.

He was staring at her with an odd, intense expression, and his eyes were bright green, the brightest green she'd ever seen. *Hello, The Good.* He kept his eyes on her as he growled out, "You're upsetting her."

Ash didn't understand. She was upsetting who?

Grim dragged a slow gaze to his Crew and said it again, much snarlier this time, "You're upsetting Ash."

"She's fine," Juno said.

"No, I'm not." Ash's eyes were burning. "I'm definitely not fine."

"What's happening?" asked a very human Brandt from where he was piling brisket onto plates for the Rogue Pride Crew.

"Nothing," Remi and Juno said in unison again. They'd turned into twins or something, and Ash was getting mad. She didn't even have an exact reason why. She just felt like the odd man out since they'd linked up in the same new crew and synced all their responses. She didn't like this. Not at all.

"Yes. Yes, something is happening," she said, glaring at the register because she was too submissive to look all the dominants in the eyes right now. "You aren't listening to me. You never listen to me."

"Who?" Remi asked.

"Both of you."

The entire Crew went still and silent, and Remi and Juno now *looked* like twins with their eyes all round like that.

Ash took a long, shaky breath. "I'm not innocent. I know what I want, and it's not some stranger-mate from bangaboarlander." Her stupid voice was so quiet, and it shook like a leaf. It made her even madder. "I want to go out with Grim." She dared a glance at him. "I want to go to the movies."

"I'll Change in a movie and probably maul seven people," Grim muttered, but that wasn't helpful so she ignored him.

She made her voice get stronger. "And I want extra butter on my popcorn. I'm going to wear the purple shirt from the picture, and I don't want anyone to update my profile anymore. I haven't taken any pictures in lingerie because I only own granny panties, and I don't know if I like butt stuff!" She clenched her hands at her sides. "But if Grim likes butt stuff, I would try it. Because I'm not innocent. And he has a very good-looking dick. I think about it a lot."

Grim's dark eyebrows disappeared under the edge of his gray beanie.

"Uh, when did you see his dick?" Remi asked.

"Last night," Grim responded. "And none of this is any of your business."

"I feel like it is my business," Rhett said, crunching on a Cheeto. "Serious question, Ash. If I gave you a measuring tape, would you measure his dick next time you see it because we have a bet going on, and I'm pretty sure mine is the longest and also the thickest, so I'm gonna need the numbers on length and also girth, and—"

"One more word, and I'll kill you," Grim deadpanned.

Rhett stopped talking immediately, zipped his lips, but then unzipped them, put another Cheeto in his mouth, and zipped it again, all while Grim stared at him with the most exhausted, slow-blinking expression Ash had ever seen. He was kind of cute when he was murdery.

"When does your shift end?" he asked.

"Um—"

"Four o'clock," Audrey called from behind a

smoker.

"But I'm not supposed to get off until six," Ash argued.

"I'm letting you off early today," Audrey said, giving Ash some serious look she didn't understand. She waggled her eyebrows. This was like reading hieroglyphics. God, people were confusing.

"But—"

"Four o'clock!" Audrey declared and marched back toward the freezer.

Okaaaay. Brandt was going to have to cover her shift. She hoped he hadn't made plans. "F-four o'clock, apparently," Ash answered Grim.

"Good. I'll pick you up from your place at five then. Is that enough time to get ready?"

"Y-yes. I don't want to smell like meat."

Grim chuckled and pushed off the counter, then sauntered toward the door.

"Where are you going?" Kamp called after him.

"I'm taking the rental car. You idiots can find your own way back to the hotel."

"You're a terrible Alpha!" Rhett called.

"Agreed," Grim said without turning around. "And yet you keep calling me your Alpha." He arched his eyebrows like they were all dumb and turned just in time to shove the exit door open and disappear outside.

Well, Ash didn't want to say goodbye yet, so she bolted around the counter and right out the front door after him. He turned in the parking lot, his eyes bright gold, a grim set to his lips.

"I know we are friends, and friends aren't supposed to just up and kiss other friends," she blurted out breathlessly. She ran the last few steps that separated them and threw her arms around his neck and pressed her lips to his. She meant to do a peck-and-release move on him, but his arms went right to her hips, gripping her hard, and his lips moved against hers. The cold wind kicked up, and between the power of the oncoming storm and the power of the man who was wrapping his arms around her, she was overwhelmed.

When he slipped his tongue past her lips, she was shocked to stillness. Her skin was tingling with the wave of dominance pulsing through her. He snarled deep in his throat as he gripped the back of her neck and whooooaaah, no one had ever kissed her like this before. Over and over, he stroked his tongue inside of her mouth until she was a panting, melting mess splayed against him.

With a soft smack, he ended the kiss but held her in place with his strong hands. Good thing, too, because her legs totally buckled and she would've hit the pavement if he wasn't holding her upright.

"I ain't a good friend," he growled through a devil-may-care smile. And then he leaned forward until his lips were right by her ear and whispered, "I fucking love the way you taste. Those are the code words." For sex? He clamped his teeth onto her earlobe until she moaned and then released her to bare her own weight on two legs that didn't want to work properly. He strode away like he knew he was king here.

And he was.

Holy balls, Ash was in trouble with that one. She grinned and swayed. Ash couldn't even remember the last time her life was this exciting. She couldn't remember the last time she felt like this about a boy. In fact, right now, watching him walk away, she couldn't quite remember anything except how to breathe, and even that was questionable because she was huffing and puffing like a winded racehorse.

Maybe Juno and Remi were right. Maybe Ash was

a little innocent. But with a teacher like Grim, she was pretty sure she wouldn't stay that way for long.

NINE

The breeze was frigid and lifted chills on Grim's forearms as he pulled on his pants.

He'd barely made it deep enough into the woods before he had to steer the SUV off the road and give the Reaper his body. The rental car was skidded sideways off the edge of some old logging road. He couldn't remember exactly how to get back down the mountain. He'd taken so many turns, desperate to find wilderness big enough for the Reaper to hunt. His clothes were scattered on the ground where he'd haphazardly thrown them in his desperation to Change.

The Reaper snarled in his throat, and Grim seized

suddenly. He staggered forward, almost went to his knees, but kept upright. Fuck. The demon in him was agitated, but hell if he knew what was wrong with him.

"You are a disaster."

Grim looked up to find a tall red-haired man leaning against the rental Ford Expedition. Vyr.

Grim didn't even try to stifle the snarl in his throat. The Reaper didn't like other dominant monsters this close. Grim balled his fists, ready.

Vyr's eyes were bright blue and had long reptilian pupils. Dragons were fuckin' creepy. The Red Dragon's attention went to Grim's fists and then to his neck. "Your burns healed well."

"Fuck you for burning me."

Vyr's lip curled up, and for a split second, his calm and collected façade slipped into something monstrous. His face twisted with rage, but then—*snap*—he looked stoic again.

"What do you want, Vyr?"

"That's a complicated question with a complicated answer. What do I want? For my people to be happy. What does my dragon want?" Vyr gave him an empty smile. "Everything."

Grim sized him up. In a fist fight, he could take him, but that damn dragon pulsing waves of power off of Vyr was a big fuckin' problem. Grim knelt by his discarded black T-shirt and pulled it over his head. Taking his eyes off the dragon for the split second the shirt covered his face dragged another snarl from the Reaper.

"The mountains my Crew lives in?" Vyr said softly. "Those are Vyr's Mountains. The mountains you and Rogue Pride live in? Those are Vyr's Mountains. Those aren't the only two. My dragon is claiming territory, and he isn't stopping like my father was able to do with his mountain range. Or Harper, or Kane, or Rowan. The Red Dragon wants it all. He wants the world."

"Why are you telling me this?"

"Because I only choose mountains where I can put a Last Chance crew with a Last Chance Alpha, so I can do good in this world, too. That's the compromise the man in me has made with the monster in me. I'm telling you so you know you aren't alone."

"I'm better off alone—"

"I remember when I thought that, too. I was full of bullshit back then. You want your inner monsters to steady out? You surround yourself with a small circle of good people. And you take care of them so you can earn their loyalty. You create a team of people who will care enough to stop you when you go off the rails. You let them bond to you, and you actually become their Alpha, not just the word. You accept the throne." Vyr lifted his chin and looked down his straight nose at Grim. "Most importantly, you let a girl in. You pick her and give your monsters something sweet to take care of. You let her *inside* of you, Grim. And then she can feed your demons light without them even knowing they're being poisoned." Vyr swallowed hard. "Do you know why I gave you the mountains, the trailer park, and the job?"

"No," Grim said, his voice breaking on the word. "I didn't even know you owned the mountains until a few months ago. I don't know why you would trust someone like me with something like that."

"Because I know your story. I made it my business to dig into the Tarian Pride after they went after Beast. You didn't show up for that battle against Kane's Crew. Why? I think I know the answer, but I want to hear it from you."

"Because it wasn't a good fight. It was stretching

our Pride too thin on a battle that didn't mean anything. Plus, fuck Justin. He deserved to die."

"Try again."

Grim swallowed hard. Fuckin' shifters and their ability to sense lies. He sighed, but it tapered into a snarl. He didn't like answering to anyone. "Because the female who ran from Justin was a girl I grew up with, and I watched him treat her like shit. She deserved a Crew like Kane's. She deserved to have a mate like Beast. I wasn't going to be the enforcer for something I didn't believe in. So while Justin and the council were going to war with Beast, I was packing up my shit and leaving the Tarian Pride. I never wanted to be a killer."

Vyr's smile was slow and unsettling. "There it is. The Reaper doesn't have as much power as you think he does. You just have to learn how to compromise with the monster."

"Yeah? And how do I do that?"

Vyr shrugged. "Ash'll do." He turned to leave, but stopped and turned back. "Oh, and Grim?"

"What?"

"You might want to give me a list of any Tarian Pride members who are worth keeping around."

Grim's heart clawed its way into his throat. "Why?"

Vyr's cold smile lifted the fine hairs on Grim's body. "Because they went after people I consider friends. I'll be claiming their mountains next."

TEN

"Do you need anything?" Juno asked as Ash removed her apron.

"Like what?"

Juno looked all frowny and worried. And behind her Remi was still hanging out at the table, too. They'd been done with their food hours ago, and Kamp and Rhett had left for the recording studio right after they finished lunch.

"Like to talk? Are you...missing anything in your life?"

"Like what?" she asked again.

Juno shrugged. "I don't know... Are you lonely?"

Okay, she needed to put a stop to whatever was

happening. Ash hung her apron on the hook behind the registers, grabbed her purse and jacket from under the counter, and marched to the table, leaving Juno to trail behind.

She plopped her perfectly cushioned ass on the bench seat across from them and pulled her jacket on. "Look. You have something to say. You are worried about something. Just tell me. You know I like things black and white. I'm not good at guessing, and this is all very...very..."

"Very what?" Remi asked in a soothing tone, arching her delicate eyebrows.

"Very frustrating!"

"Well, I can imagine so. Grim isn't easy to—"

"I'm not frustrated with Grim. You two are acting so weird."

"Not weird," Juno argued. "Protective."

"Really? Because when you told me about Rhett, I supported you right away. And when you told me about Kamp," she said, jamming a finger at Remi, "what did I say immediately? Without even waiting a second, what did I say?"

"That you were happy for me."

Ash huffed a breath and then plopped her chin

onto her folded arms on the table. "Then you owe me. Be happy for me."

Juno scrubbed her hands down her face and growled. "It's not that easy, Ash. You're...you're...and Grim is...well he's..."

"Just say it."

"You're too good for him."

Ash shook her head, digging her chin into her wrist. "You never just say what you mean with me. And it used to be okay because I just wanted you to keep liking me. And so I was quiet when something bothered me."

"Oh my gosh," Remi said in a small voice. "Like what things? What things weren't okay?"

"The way you talk for me sometimes. Like when we are out and someone pays attention to me, you talk for me. I used to like it because it meant I didn't have to talk or try to be smart to other people, but right now, I don't like it. You both moved away, but I'm still here, and I...changed. I don't need you to talk for me anymore, but you still do it when you come back home."

Both of her friends were quiet and exchanged a glance that said something big, but one she didn't understand.

"I know I'm simple," she murmured. "I know it. I know I'm submissive. I barely graduated high school because stuff is so confusing. But I do know how to talk. For myself. And I know the things I want."

"What things?" Remi asked quietly.

Grim. "A mate someday. If you block me from anything real, I'll never find it."

"You think Grim is real?"

Ash shrugged. "He feels different."

"But…he's, well…" Remi said, struggling. "He's bad, Ash."

"Only half-bad, same as everyone else. I got bad in me. I got hungry at lunch and wanted to steal a sandwich before I even paid for it. Bad. You drank whiskey before you were even eighteen, and me and Juno had to hold your hair back while you got sick in the men's bathroom because the women's bathroom was all full and that was a gross night. Bad. Juno, you got all wrapped in your career like duct tape and stopped visiting your parents for a long time and they got sad. Bad. You both left me." Ash's eyes filled suddenly with tears and her lip trembled, so she buried her face in her arms to hide her crying. Her voice broke on the word, "Bad."

"Aw, shhhhit," Remi muttered.

Ash was going to get it all out, all the poison in her mind, because if she didn't do it now, she never would. She couldn't look up at them, though, or she would turn chicken-bear, so she just talked into her arms instead. "You both went and got big lives and you stopped calling me and you stopped telling me your inside jokes and you left me behind. I still existed while you were away. I waited. I was happy for you both, but I waited because I wanted things to go back to when it was just the three of us running around here. But you left, and it made me be more independent. And then right when I was getting used to being more independent, you come back and speak for me again."

"You really like Grim?" Remi asked.

"Yes. And I can tell he likes me, too."

"How?"

"Because his good lion watches me."

"Wait, what?" Juno asked.

Ash sniffed and wiped her eyes on her sleeve. She probably had mascara smeared everywhere now, but she didn't care. "The green-eyed one. He comes out for me."

"Grim doesn't have green eyes," Remi whispered. "He has brown eyes and he has gold eyes."

"The good part of Grim does have green eyes," Ash assured them. "You just haven't seen them. I do."

Now Juno and Remi looked as confused as Ash always felt. "Huh," Juno puffed out on a breath.

"And look." Ash pulled out her phone and showed them the first picture that popped up in her Grim the Hottie album. It was the one where he was chopping wood. "He did this without me even asking him to. When we were hanging out at the firepit last night, we ran out of wood, so he got up early before I took him back to town and chopped more wood. I snuck this picture."

Juno and Remi stared at the picture with eyes that were round as pepperonis.

"Okay," Remi said.

"Okay?" Juno asked her.

Remi nodded and looked back at Ash, then gave another nod. "Yeah. If Grim hurts her, we'll just kill him."

"Yeah. Okay, we'll just kill our Alpha, no big deal," Juno said.

"Then it's settled," Ash said. "No more speaking for me, okay?"

"Deal," said Juno.

Remi's lips curved into a smile.

"What?" Ash asked.

"Well...I'm just so proud of you."

"Me, too," Juno said. "This is a side of you we haven't seen before. Good for you, Ash. You should go get the life you want. And we shouldn't be standing in the way of anything. That's not what friends do."

"And we are friends," Ash said with a nod. She wiped her damp cheeks. "Best friends. Things are different, but we are still best friends. You will always be my best friends."

Juno and Remi reached for her hand at the same time and clutched it hard.

Remi's eyes were leaking. "Yeah."

"Always," murmured Juno.

ELEVEN

She was definitely being stood up.

Ash wrung her hands again to warm them and blew out a long, frozen breath. It was really cold sitting out here on the front porch. She loved stormy days and gray clouds and usually she didn't get cold easy, but she was nervous, and that wasn't helping.

She'd dressed in layers, her purple sweater, leggings, snow boots, a jacket, and a scarf that was the same shade of blue as her hair. She'd done her make-up like those internet videos she'd watched after Juno and Remi left Damon's Mountains and everything got boring. She was pretty good at eyeliner now but not contouring her cheekbones.

That was witchcraft and rocket science.

He'd said five o'clock, and she'd been sitting out here for a whole hour. She should probably go inside, heat up a TV dinner, watch a movie, and try to forget about how much her chest was hurting right now.

Boys did that when they threw girls away. They hurt them in their chests. She'd wanted Grim to be different, though.

"Goodnight, Wanda," she muttered to her ancient charcoal-gray Dodge Ram pickup. Her dad had given her his old truck for her sixteenth birthday, and they still fixed it together when it broke down. She would never get rid of it because she and Dad had put so much love into keeping the old girl running.

Sad down to her bone marrow, Ash stood and made her way across the creaking front porch to her front door. But right as she reached for the handle, the soft hum of a car engine sounded.

And just like that, the hole in her chest filled with hope.

The sound got closer and closer. She lived out in the middle of nowhere, so it had to be him. She arranged her face to be mad because he was very late and shouldn't be greeted with a smile when he did something wrong.

He parked right in front of the house in the SUV rental and shoved open the door. "I know I'm late. I'm so sorry."

"Why?"

Grim was wearing the same black T-shirt that clung to his powerful shoulders, the sleeves of his blue flannel were rolled up to his elbows. The gray beanie was pulled low on his forehead, and his skin was paler than she remembered. The black tattoos on his neck looked so dark next to his white skin. His eyes were hollow, and he looked unwell.

But all he said in answer was, "There's no excuse good enough to make up for being an hour late, Ash. Light me up."

Like a glowstick? "I don't know what that means."

"You can yell at me."

"Did you Change?"

He ducked his gaze, and that was answer enough.

"Into the Reaper?"

He nodded slightly.

"Well...I suppose that's okay then. You aren't easy, are you? This is one of those times when I have to decide if I accept the bad part or leave, right?"

Grim inhaled deeply. "Yeah. You'll have a lot of those moments with me. And if you leave, I'll understand. It's okay."

She canted her head and studied him. In his hand was clutched a small paper bag. "Did you bring me a present?"

He huffed a relieved-sounding chuckle and closed the distance between them. He handed her the bag.

"I really love presents," she whispered, giving up on trying to hide her smile. "And I missed you and thought you didn't want to see me anymore. I really wanted to go to a movie tonight." She opened the paper bag and gasped at the present inside. It was a tiny flower pot, no bigger than a golf ball. On the packaging was a picture of miniature pink roses.

"It has everything you need to start growing the roses in that tiny pot. When they get big enough, you can transplant them into the yard. And I'll kill anyone who rips them up."

"Ooooh," she said on a breath, holding the tiny pot and crinkling paper bag to her chest. "This is my favorite present."

He searched her face with an awed look she didn't understand.

"What?" she asked, worried.

"You just look so pretty when you smile like that. Your cheeks go all pink. I think they turn pink when you're happy."

Wow. No one had ever looked that closely at her. Now her cheeks were probably getting even pinker. "I like being happy," she whispered.

"I know. I can tell. It's just...well, I'm not usually the one that makes anyone happy."

"Well, you do that for me," she said with a nod. "I'm going to grow pretty roses and cut off the thorns and send some to your grandma."

Grim wasn't even growling right now. That was new. He was just smiling. He pulled her in for a warm hug that smushed her boobs against his stony chest and made her feel all fluttery inside.

Boys could make a girl's chest hurt, sure. But they could also fill them up with butterflies, and butterflies were her favorite bug.

Grim swallowed hard. "You asked if it hurt."

"The Good and The Bad?"

"Yeah." Grim held her closer and swayed with her. "Yes, it hurts."

"All the time?"

"Yes."

"Oh, Grim." She rested her cheek against his chest and scratched his back gently as they rocked. "If I could take it away for a little while, I would."

"Really?"

"Of course. It must be very hard to stay steady when you get pulled like that. Tug of war for you all the time. In my head, I get mad at my bear when she is too submissive. I wish she was different sometimes. And you have two different ones." She looked up into his face and touched his beard lightly. "You are very strong, Grim."

He chuckled darkly and shook his head. "Wrong," he said, using her word from last night at the bar. "Why would you think that, woman? I want to kill everything. I want to fight everything. I can't stand the man I am. I can't stand the animal I am. I can't stop my Changes, I can't do my job, and I can't be an Alpha for my Crew. I can't keep you. I know I can't. And I want to. It's the first thing I've really wanted in I-don't-even-know-how-long. And it makes me angry. Makes me pissed I can't have one thing I want."

"But you can."

"Ash, you're breakable. It's not your job to fix a

monster. You'll lose some of the things I like about you. You'll have to accept things when you deserve better. And you'll compromise over and over until you realize how unfair it is that I picked you. I like you a lot. I like you enough to know you deserve much better than where I'm headed."

Ash huffed a breath and tugged his beard. "Are you done tryin' to leave?"

He froze, looking utterly stunned that his beard had been accosted, but so what? He was being ridiculous.

"This is a boring talk," she assured him. "Doesn't change anything. I still want to be around you tonight. And probably tomorrow night. And probably the next night until your Crew makes you go back to your mountains. And then I'll be very sad and wait to see if you message my bangaboarlander page. I'll imagine what your life is like there and make ten-ten wishes that you find happy moments. Because you deserve them."

Grim shook his head, back and forth, back and forth, but she pressed her fingertips tighter against his cheeks to keep him in place.

"You don't see me right," he whispered.

"Maybe it's everyone else who doesn't see you right."

He swallowed hard and moved away from her. He angled his face at the SUV in her driveway. "Come on, Good Girl. You're shivering, and there are butt-warmers in the truck. I don't like when you're cold."

As she walked beside him, she slipped her hand into his because she was figuring him out. He wasn't as worried about her being cold as he was about her words. She was breaking him down a little. Why? Because Ash knew no one had been nice to him like this. No one had ever told him he was worth anything more than an enforcer for a bunch of heartless monster lions. But he was so, so, soooo much more. He was still here. Still fighting. Tough man. She respected that way more than a man who'd buckled under the darkness and quit. Who'd given in. Grim wasn't a quitter. She'd never figured out someone this easily. He was like a book. He had triumphant chapters and scary chapters. Right now, the triumphant chapters were short and the scary ones long. But that was okay because, for once, she was good at reading. For her, every interaction with people was confusing and hard. Every day was the same. But Grim had come in and made sense to her. She felt relieved around him. And she didn't want him to leave. So...she was going to keep breaking up his scary chapters with the nice words she thought because, no matter how strong a man was, he should hear the good.

Grim squeezed her hand, and when he looked down at her, his eyes were a brilliant green. *Hello, The Good.* He was telling her thank you for being nice to him. For being understanding. Those green eyes were a reward. She understood his thank you. It was another sentence of his book that she could read.

"What kind of music do you like?" he asked as she buckled herself into the passenger's seat.

"Uuuuum," she drawled out as she rested her fingertips against the vent blasting warm air. "I like the music on the one-oh-eight-point-five station."

Grim hit the seek button on the radio until it settled on the station. A Youngbloodz song was playing its first chorus. She mouthed the lyrics and bobbed her head to the fast beat as she stared out the window at the snowy woods blurring by.

Grim laughed, and it sounded surprised, so she looked over at him to try to understand. He took his eyes off the road long enough to look at her with a big what-the-hell grin, then back to the road, then back to her. Ash's cheeks felt hot again, so she ducked her gaze and scrunched up her nose in embarrassment.

"No, no, no, woman, sing it. Do you know the lyrics?"

Ash nodded. "I have a good memory."

"Rap," he demanded. Usually, if someone told her to do something so directly, she would wiggle away from it unless it was her dad, her boss, Audrey, or the Alpha she'd grown up with, Harrison. But Grim looked like he was impressed with her, so she whispered the next two lines of lyrics.

"Do it louder."

She giggled and then inhaled deep. Then, at normal volume, she finished the verse, and when Grim joined her on the chorus, she cracked up through the first two lines. His voice was good for rap. Nice and gritty, and he seemed to have a good memory, too. She liked this. She liked this very much. So she lifted her voice and danced in her seat and sang every word of the rest of the song.

"Who *are* you?" he asked, his smile lighting up his whole face.

Well…no one had ever asked her that before, and it drew her up short. Who *was* she? "I'm Ash Bear, the daughter of Bash Bear, barbecue maker, bestie to Juno and Remi, under the protection of Damon Daye, and apparently Vyr Daye if the mostly-healed burn on your neck is anything to go by. I cook, rap, have blue hair and big curves, and like being happy. And I'm a bad talker, but I want to be better, so I keep trying."

"Listen to you, Ash. You talk fine with me. You can work on anything you want, but I don't see a single thing wrong with the way you talk."

"Well, it's different and easy with you," she said softly.

An old-school song came on the radio then. Grim and Ash both said, "Oooooooooh!" and then burst out laughing before they could catch the third line of the first verse.

Grim danced in his seat with her, and he grinned so big when he hit a good lyric. Tattoos, huge muscles, and a mohawk spiked up just right, *and* he smelled like hot-guy cologne. Or deodorant. She couldn't tell which. He was so, so, soooo pretty.

Her heart pounded hard as they sang together. She didn't care if she missed lyrics or mumbled through a line. She was having so much fun she didn't even notice that Grim had taken a wrong turn and missed the road for the movie theater in Saratoga. She didn't notice anything until he pulled into the parking lot of Sammy's Bar. It was early, only 6:30, so the gravel parking lot was mostly empty. Only a few cars were parked on the side, and one of them was Layla's, the owner of the bar.

"I know you wanted to go to the movies," Grim said, backing the car into a parking spot like he'd gotten a college degree in car reversing. "But I can't do a theater. I know what I am and am not capable of, and being on a plane to get here was literally hell on my animals. Being in a crowded movie theater is a recipe for disaster. I would rather not traumatize you and every human in there for our first date."

"Oh." *He said date, he said date!* Ash reached over and patted his thigh. "It's okay Reaper and The Good. We can go to the bar instead. They have delicious chicken wings, four for a dollar tonight. We can eat like sixteen chickens' worth and play more pool or something."

Grim put the SUV in park and relaxed back against the headrest, staring at her with pretty green eyes. The Good was bigger than Grim had said he was. "You're an accepter, aren't you?"

"What do you mean?"

"Doesn't matter if I fail at something, you don't pout or get disappointed in me. You just find something else to focus on."

"Yeah, that sounds like me."

"It's a rare thing to find, Ash. In a good way. Most people would make me pay every time I fuck up, but I don't think that'll be how you handle hanging out with me. You're gonna make it hard to hate myself, aren't you?"

"Yes, that definitely sounds like me."

He chuckled a warm sound that vibrated through her veins and landed in her chest. That's maybe what joy sounded like. She wished she could bottle it up in a jar and keep it in her purse, listen to it when she got confused by people. It would make everything better.

"I know it's not a real theater, but I talked to Layla, and she's letting me use the screen and projector equipment left over from Rhett's concert.

Wide-eyed, Ash looked behind them at Sammy's Bar, and sure enough, the screen was still set up. It took up half the old brick wall.

"I asked Juno what your favorite movie was," Grim admitted, pushing the door open. He jogged around the front of the SUV and opened her door for her.

"My favorite movie is *Empire Records*," she murmured, completely stunned.

Grim reached over her lap and unbuckled her, then stopped, his lips right near to hers. "I know. I got it from the store where I got the roses. And popcorn, the movie-theater-butter kind." He leaned in and kissed her so gently she melted. That's the only word that could describe her right now. She slipped her hands to his neck and moved her lips against his. Grim moaned softly, and that tiny noise lit every nerve ending in her body on fire. Oooh, she liked him. And he liked her. She could tell. "You really did all this for me?" she asked against his lips.

She could taste his smile. He kissed her again, a soft peck, and then locked his arms against the edge of the seat and leveled her with brown eyes. For a moment, they were normal. It was just Ash and Joshua. Two people having their first big date, falling for each other, or at least that's what it felt like when she kissed him. Like her stomach was dipping from a roller coaster ride. Grim was the loop-de-loop. And the loop-de-loop was her favorite part of roller coasters.

"Come on," he murmured, offering her his hand like a real gentleman. No one would've expected a man who looked like him to be a gentleman, but she knew better than to judge a book by its cover. He was a great book.

She followed him to the rear of the SUV where he opened the back. As the door lifted slowly, it exposed a pile of blankets. The last row of seats had been folded down, making a place to sit.

"I'm gonna pop the popcorn and grab us a drink," he murmured, blowing frozen breath into his hands.

"Will you tuck me in?" she asked.

He canted his head, studying her for a second, and then nodded toward the blankets. "Get on in."

Ash crawled in the back, breathless and giggly and her cheeks all warm. From happiness, she supposed, like Grim said. She plopped her tooshie right up against the middle row of seats as her back rest and then enjoyed the butterflies as he covered her in blankets and tucked them all around her. He straightened her beanie, pressed his forehead against hers with a little growl in his throat, and sauntered off toward the projector. He fiddled with it for a few seconds. The previews started up on the screen, but she couldn't take her eyes off his back as he jogged toward Sammy's. Black shirt, dark jeans, scuffed-up tan work boots, and that raven-black hair. The thin layer of pristine white snow in the parking lot made him look so dark.

She really, really liked him. It wasn't just her either. Her inner bear sat right under her skin watching him, too. Mesmerized with him. Awed perhaps. Definitely taken with Grim. Even after the door closed behind him, she found it hard to pay attention to the previews playing on the wall of Sammy's. Her attention stayed rivetted on the doorknob as she and her bear waited for Grim to come back. She didn't much like being separated, even for buttery popcorn. A growl scratched up her throat. *It's okay bear. He'll be back soon.*

And he was. Five minutes later, and he was cradling two cups of steaming hot chocolate against his ribs with one arm and a bowl of popcorn in the other.

That was her man. Hot chocolate and popcorn

and a smile just for her. And his soft brown human eyes. Her heart skipped a beat.

The movie started just as he got to the SUV, and she pulled the edge of the blankets up for him. He got all situated and adjusted, right up next to her. How was a man this warm? Even for a shifter, he ran hot. He was like a six-foot-four, muscle-bound furnace. She wanted to do bad stuff with him, but snuggling was good for now.

About ten minutes, half a bowl of popcorn, and her entire cup of hot chocolate later, something kinda cool happened. The sun was setting and the movie showed up better against the screen, and just as Grim slipped his arm around her shoulders, the door to Sammy's opened. Ash gasped with surprise but also happiness. Her best friends were here. Remi and Juno piled out of Sammy's with Kamp and Rhett following, both talking to each other too low for Ash to hear over the sound of the song from the music store scene. Remi looked back at the movie and then at the SUV. She squinted and then smiled really big as she waved. "Ash!"

"Oh my gosh, is this what you guys meant by movie night?" Juno called, jogging with Remi toward them.

"Fantastic," Grim muttered, but he had a tiny smile pulling at the corners of his lips that said he wasn't that mad the Rogue Pride Crew was crashing their date.

"I'll get the truck," Kamp said, "that we had to borrow because some asshole stole the rental car." He didn't sound that mad, though, as he jogged toward an old Ford that looked like Tagan's of the Ashe Crew.

The sound of the engine reached them as Juno, Remi, and Rhett stomped snow off their boots near the SUV.

"If you're going to watch this with us, you have to shut the fuck up," Grim muttered.

He was so cute when he cursed.

"Wait..." Rhett whispered, his eyes going round as a pea on a plate. "Did you just invite us to movie night?"

"No," Grim said, never taking his eyes from the screen.

"But I think you did," Rhett murmured. "I knew it would happen. I knew it all along."

"Shhhh!" Grim demanded.

"We just became best friends," Rhett said, stooping. He picked up a pair of snow-covered pebbles and handed one to Grim. "Put this in your pocket so you can remember this moment for always."

"Fuck. Off." Grim grabbed the small rock and chucked it into the parking lot. He enlightened Rhett with, "You're standing directly in the way. As usual."

Rhett canted his head and looked mushy. "I love you, too."

A ferocious growl vibrated Grim's entire body as he dragged his bright gold gaze to Rhett, who suddenly looked like he'd sucked on a lemon. He took three deliberate steps to the side.

After Kamp backed the borrowed truck right up next to the SUV, Juno ripped one of the thick blankets from their legs, grabbed a handful of popcorn, kissed Ash on the cheek with a loud smack, and then she and the others of Rogue Pride situated themselves in the back of the truck beside them.

And that wasn't the only cool thing that happened. A pair of headlights shone against the wall before another truck backed in on their other side. It was one of the humans in town, Davis Mauro. "Hey all. I just got off work and was driving by. Saw the movie playing. It's a good one. Mind if I watch, too?"

She thought Grim would say no, but he didn't. He just nodded and went back to watching. Good Reaper being nice and quiet tonight. She slid her hand on top of his thigh under the covers as a reward, and it was the first time she heard Grim purr. She'd been wrong about his chuckle being what joy sounded like. It was this, his animal's satisfied purr. Gooood, goooood Reaper.

And they kept coming—the headlights. Headlights and cars, filling up the parking lot of Sammy's one by one. Some people went inside, but most stayed right out here, watching the movie. Some got out of their cars and stood outside in heavy jackets, all paired up, talking low and laughing at the funny parts. It was hard to watch the movie because everyone seemed to be having so much fun.

"This is the coolest night," she whispered excitedly.

Grim pulled her closer and looked around at the makeshift party. "It is? I was afraid your movie night was getting ruined."

"No! Look what you did, Grim." She twisted in the

seat so she could look out the front window at the cars filtering into the parking lot. "These people are coming here to spend time together and watch a movie. You gave the people in this town a fun night. Look! There's some of the Gray Back Crew right there!" Willa's fiery red hair and echoing laugh as she hung out the window of her truck and waved were impossible to miss.

"And this is all a good thing?" he asked in a gravelly voice.

Ash turned back around and snuggled closer into his ribs. "I like it very much."

"I talked to Vyr today," he said suddenly in a soft voice.

Ash checked his burns again on instinct. She brushed her fingertips across the raised pink marks that would probably look like nothing in a few days, thanks to his super-healing. No new burns so it must've been a civil talk.

"He said I should be a better Alpha."

"Do you want to be? Better, I mean?"

Grim shook his head and then sighed. "I never wanted to be an Alpha. I can barely keep my own shit together, but for better or worse, those idiots have stuck with me. I keep trying to kill them, and they keep surviving. Now I'm starting to think I'm stuck with them."

Grim was very cute when he was grumpy.

"Well, you're lucky then. They are like little love-barnacles on the tail of a beluga whale—"

"Great white shark," he corrected her.

"Of a great white shark...and sometimes they say offensive stuff, but they smile when they call you names to let you know they really care. It's good to have a Crew like that."

Grim gritted his teeth so hard his jaw twitched. And then he muttered, "Do you want to sit in the truck with them?"

"Yes!"

And as he gathered up their blankets and the popcorn, she poured out of the back like a ladle of gravy because one of her legs had fallen asleep. But she didn't mind because tonight was amazing. Rogue Pride was calling to them and waving them over, and Grim was growling quietly, as if he didn't mind that much.

As he helped her onto the tailgate, she told him, "I'm really glad you aren't a great white shark shifter because I'm not good at swimming...and sex would be very difficult...and our love story would be very short on account of me drowning."

Grim froze for a one-count, his hands gripping her hips as she sat on the edge of the truck. And then he let out a great echoing laugh.

"Oh my God, that was awesome," Rhett said from behind them.

The others were laughing, too, and she didn't really know what she'd said that was funny, but she did know one thing—every time Grim laughed or purred, he made her heart happier.

They scrambled into the back of the truck. There wasn't much room because the males in this Crew were silly amounts of gigantic, but she sat in Grim's warm lap like Juno and Remi did with their mates. It was more comfortable for her butt cheeks. Plus, while they laughed at the movie and joked around with each other, Ash got to feel Grim's glorious boner against her tailbone, and everything was finally, finally right with the world.

She looked around at her friends that she'd missed so much. At their easy smiles and banter, at their mates who looked at the Remi and Juno like they were the stars and the moon and glitter and pizza rolls and all of the other best things in the world. Grim's hand was resting lightly on her hip, his eyes sometimes green, sometimes gold, but mostly steady brown on her and her smile. Her favorite movie was playing in the background, and they were sharing the last of the popcorn like they were all old friends. The soft murmur of happy voices all around them was a song for her soul. She'd been so lonely when Remi and Juno had left, but tonight, right now, she couldn't even remember what loneliness felt like.

This was magic and all made possible because Grim wanted to give her a special night.

She should tell him her nice thoughts because even strong men should know when they've done something right.

"Tonight is my favorite night of all nights, and it's all because of you."

He looked surprised in a good way, and his eyes flashed that pretty green color for just a few moments. Then he pulled her close against his chest, leaned back against the metal of the truck bed, and murmured against her ear. "Mine, too. Because of you."

TWELVE

The movie was through and the cars were starting to disappear from the parking lot in front of Sammy's. Everyone seemed distracted, so maybe now was a good time.

Over and over again, Grim had looked at that lone pebble that sat near the front sidewalk of the bar. Rhett had kept his, and Grim had this stupid urge to pocket the one he'd given him. Why? Because, apparently, he'd turned into a sentimental pussy cat. The Tarian Pride would kill him on principle if they ever found out how weak he was now.

He tried to ignore it, but the damn pebble kept talking to him in Rhett's voice.

"Grim."

"Grimleton."

"Grimapotamus."

"Grimmy Grim Grim."

Stupid fucking rock.

And stupid fucking Grim for being a legitimate psychopath who made up words for a rock in his least favorite friend's voice.

Rhett was a canker sore.

But as much as he didn't trust Vyr, the Red Dragon had made some fair points earlier. One of them being that he should maybe try to be a better Alpha. Or at the very least, let the Rogue Pride Crew in a little bit.

So when everyone was distracted with gathering the blankets and the popcorn bowl, he strode over to the dumb pebble, stooped down to pick it up, and pocketed it as fast as he could.

He shoved his hands deep in his pockets and made his way back to the SUV, only daring to glance up once. Everyone was busy and hadn't paid attention to what he'd done except for Ash, who wore the prettiest smile he'd ever seen.

Of course, he had to stop and kiss her just to taste

how sweet she was.

And when he cast a glance at Rhett, he caught the Rogue Pride jokester looking at him with an expression he didn't understand. Busted, Rhett looked away fast and busied himself with folding a blanket.

Grim held out his arm for Ash so she wouldn't slip on the ice, and led her back to the passenger side of the SUV as she called her goodbyes over her shoulder. She was so damn cute. And confident talking to the others. It was a big difference from the way she'd been last night. Maybe she just didn't like being in big crowds, but a selfish part of him hoped she was more confident because she knew she was safe with him. Seriously, *seriously* safe. He would gut anyone who even looked at her wrong.

Grim jogged around the back of the SUV as the Crew was climbing into the borrowed pickup truck.

Old Grim would've gotten into his ride, rolled down the window like he was about to say something nice, then flip them off and peel out hard enough to throw snow all over them.

But Ash would be disappointed if he did that, so New Grim tried to ignore them instead. But then he thought she would be disappointed in that, too, so he kicked the tire and snarled as he spun around. The entire Crew jumped in unison as he barked out, "Listen up, you cretins." He cleared his throat and lifted his chin higher. "Tonight wasn't terrible."

And then he got in the SUV and drove away, only looking in the rearview mirror once to witness Rhett standing in the middle of the parking lot waving to him and wearing this dumb, mushy smile like he'd just seen the birth of his first kid.

So Grim rolled down the window and flipped him off.

Baby steps.

THIRTEEN

Grim was starting to feel different from the inside out.

It was terrifying.

He'd been exactly the same for so long he didn't know how to do this...this...changing thing. But the beautiful girl beside him had turned everything inside out.

She made him feel salvageable. Oh, he wasn't a sentimental man. The opposite really. He was a realist and had known from the day the Reaper was born that he would only live a half-life. No real friends, no mate, no cubs, no future. He was cursed to live in the moment and hope to God he could keep the

Reaper under control enough to make it to the next moment, and the next and the next.

Rinse and repeat until his last breath which, honestly, he'd figured would come from one of the Rogue Pride Crew or from Vyr himself.

Yet here he was, still breathing, and not only that, but he was feeling emotions a monster like him had no business feeling.

He should run...right?

He should leave this little siren alone before he became addicted to the way she made him feel. Before he got protective and defensive and claimed her. Before he ruined her life.

But sitting here in the SUV, vents blasting warm air on them, Ash holding onto his arm and singing softly to a hip hop song, he couldn't even imagine walking away.

Not for himself, and not for the benefit of her either.

And that, right there, was proof he was a monster. A selfish one. One who put the little glimpse of happiness he felt before her safety.

The Reaper was here, waiting and watching her. Hunting her maybe, he didn't know. Nothing made sense except he liked this high she gave him.

Hope.

He startled slightly. He still wasn't used to the good lion's voice yet.

Ash had both arms wrapped around his bicep as he rested his free hand on her thigh. She kissed his arm softly, and his heart rate raced a little less. She was a drug. Whatever made Ash Ash, spoke to him in a way that no one else ever had.

He was a chipped and damaged wrecking ball destined to always be just that, a destroyer, but tonight he'd watched her laugh and smile and tell him nice things that made him have moments where he thought, *I can do this. I can be okay for her.*

Was this just The Good talking? Was the good lion just so desperate to hold onto all the face time he could get that he would endanger Ash to have it?

He trusted his animals about zero percent. Maybe less.

He pulled to a stop in front of her little cabin. She'd left the front porch light on, and the little place looked homey. But a sudden homesickness washed over him, and it rocked him back a bit.

"I wish I could show you my den."

"In the trailer park? In the Oregon mountains?"

Grim turned off the car and relaxed back. "Yeah. I wish I could show you my life. My mess of a life. Show you all the bad parts to test you and see how fast you run."

"I'm not a huge fan of cardio, Grim."

He snorted, and then another chuckle escaped him. She was smiling, so she knew she was being funny this time. She was so damn cute. The perfect combination of sexy, adorable, and funny. It was a hard balance to manage for a person, but she did it flawlessly.

He'd never felt this way about any person.

"I don't know how to pair up or take care of a woman," he admitted.

"You took care of me just fine today," she said with a shrug.

Fuck, he couldn't believe he was about to tell her this. It was a big admission. "In the Tarian Pride, after the Reaper was born, they made a rule for me."

"I don't like that. You're a king. Why would a king have to mind rules?" Her voice was lower and had grit to it. Good girl. Protective she-grizzly.

"My value to the Pride was as an enforcer. I had

no choice. I was wrecked, had very little control, couldn't live with another Pride the way I was. They would have killed me as soon as they figured out how damaged I was. I was one of those lions you put down, not keep. The rule was that I wasn't allowed to have a female. They were afraid a female would soften me, and I wouldn't be as useful to them."

"For fighting?"

"Yes. I built a reputation. The Reaper loved the fight, and I didn't lose. Not after he was born. Most of the time I could just show up in a territory, and we could claim it. The shifters there would feel my attention on them, feel me hunting them, and they would pack up and leave. I fed the Reaper on the blood of those fights."

"No, no, no. The Tarian Pride fed the Reaper."

Grim ran his hands over his mohawk and sighed. "I wanted companionship, but the females were kept away from me. Everyone was kept away from me. I lived a solitary life so I would stay angry. So I would keep the chip they'd carved into my shoulder. I only left that pride six months ago." He shrugged and shook his head. "I don't know how to take care of something fragile."

"Okay, well, that has nothing to do with me."

"What?"

"I'm not fragile." There was such pure honesty in those three words. It was something she knew to be true about herself, and it made him think.

What was fragile? Was it smiling and enjoying life and appreciating the simple things? No. Was it submissiveness? No, he'd never seen that as a weakness either. His grandma was submissive, but she'd been steadfast and strong and taken every awful and hurtful word the Tarian Pride had fed her and swallowed it down, and then lived her life despite them. For a second, he'd been mistaken that Ash was weak because she was choosing to be around him, a walking disaster. But perhaps that showed Ash's strength, not weakness, to know in her heart he was part monster and stick beside him anyway.

"Can I sleep here tonight?" he asked.

She set her teeth to his bicep gently, and a purr ripped from his throat as he rolled his eyes closed with how good it felt.

"Only if you sleep in bed with me."

"I have to leave tomorrow," he admitted before he

could change his mind. He should've just left without telling her and let her keep her normal life here, but he was selfish, remember?

"But Rhett said he had two more days of recording," she said, sitting up straight.

Her eyes were so blue, her cheeks a pretty pink to match the lip gloss on her pout. Beautiful girl. He would give what was left of his soul to keep her.

"Vyr is claiming territory. He has his eyes on the Tarian Pride's mountains. It's a big territory, but I don't trust the Red Dragon. My grandma is there. I need to get her out before he pushes to take over. Before he burns the damn mountains and eats the ashes." Oh, he'd seen the news footage. He knew exactly how a dragon claimed mountains. The border of the territory would be burned to ash, eaten, and then the stink of dragon's smoke would cling to the land. It clung to the mountains in Oregon where he lived.

"But...Vyr is good."

"Is he?"

"Yes," she said, a frown furrowing her perfectly arched dark eyebrows. "He's good. I know these things. I can feel them. I grew up with him, and I know how he is now. He's got a good Crew, a good mate. They'll keep him steady. He's okay."

But Grim couldn't be sure. Vyr had admitted to compromising with his monster, and Grim knew all about inner monsters. There wasn't real compromise. They sat inside of a man until they fancied destruction, and then they mauled everything. And Vyr wasn't some lion that was easily put down. He was a motherfucking dragon. Grim didn't trust him where his grandma's safety was concerned. He didn't trust anyone except Ash.

"Rose is special," she murmured about his grandma.

She'd remembered his grandma's name. "Yes. She's very special to me."

Ash dropped those pretty blues to her hands clasped tightly in her lap. "Then you should go. Tomorrow. Bring her somewhere safe so your lions can stay calm and settled."

Smart girl. She was so much more clever than she realized.

"Will you stay with me tonight?" she asked.

He hated that she was looking away, so he gently pulled her face back to him. What he saw in her eyes gutted him. They were rimmed with tears. Sweet bear. "I told you I would hurt you."

She hugged him tight and buried her face against his chest. "It's okay. It's okay."

Fuck, what was this awful feeling in his chest? Guilt? His damn heart hurt. He was gonna miss the hell out of her. Out of this feeling...whatever it was.

So right here and now, he decided he was going to take her mind off of separating and give her a good last night. He was going to force the Reaper to stay in his skin for one night, and he was going to hold Ash while she slept. For one tiny little night, he was going to pretend they were normal, that he was strong and deserved someone as inherently good as Ash.

She'd told him tonight was her favorite of all her nights, and he was going to make sure that stayed true for her.

Tonight, he was damn determined they would be just Grim and Ash.

Even if it meant swallowing the pain of The Reaper.

Because taking care of her felt more important than taking care of himself.

And that, he realized, was the good lion inside of

him speaking up again.

The clock changed to 10:10. The blue numbers sat there taunting him, glowing, beckoning him. Juno and Remi did this dumb thing where they wished on the number. Something about an old trailer that was magic in Damon's Mountains. Wishes weren't granted for devils like him, but he could feel that small, quiet, green-eyed goodness watching Ash. The Good would keep her safe. He would help Grim fight the Reaper tonight if it made Ash happy.

The Good cared about her smiles.

As the final seconds of the minute ticked by, he pressed his finger to the clock and closed his eyes, gripped Ash tighter against him with his other hand, and for the first time in his life, he made a wish.

I wish The Good would stay.

FOURTEEN

Ash had watched him place his fingertip on the number 10:10 and close his eyes. He'd made a wish. A man who didn't believe in magic had made a wish. A hopeless man had wished for something.

Ash rushed and put her finger on top of his, closed her eyes, and made a wish for him.

I wish The Good would stay.

Then Grim wouldn't hurt so bad on his insides.

She did believe in magic, and she did have hope, and for the rest of always, no matter where they ended up, she was going to do her best to give Grim hope, too. Because he deserved happiness, peace, and to be steady. Or as steady as a man like him could be.

When she opened her eyes, Grim was watching her with an unreadable expression. His eyes were so bright green.

She loved him. She was a silly girl who had fallen in love with a boy in a day. One day, and her heart had just decided that it belonged to him, her Grim. It had recognized his heart, pointed to him, and said, "That's mine." She didn't have many people, so her bear became very loyal and protective to the ones she did have. She wasn't anything special. A submissive bear shifter who was easily confused, but no matter what, Grim was safe with her. He would always have someone at his back, even when he left and moved on to live his life. She would always be there if he needed someone. If he needed anything.

The Good. The Bad. It was all hers, and there was nothing he could ever do to change her mind. She told him, "Even if someday you admitted to me all the bad things you had to do as the knife of the Tarian Pride, I'll listen, and then I'll hold those memories with you. You can tell me anything, and I won't think less of you. I won't make you pay for your past."

"What are you saying?" he asked softly.

"You're safe."

Grim ripped his gaze away from her fast and stared out the window on the other side. He was hiding from her—another line of his book that she could read. Men did that sometimes, the strong ones. They hid when their hearts were touched. He'd probably never heard those words before, so he couldn't tell if they hurt or if they felt good.

So she wrapped her arms around his bicep again and rubbed her cheek against the goosebumps on his skin. He didn't feel cold, but he had chills. Poor Grim. She didn't like when he had chills. She kissed his arm, right over a tattoo. Then suddenly, he leaned forward and yanked the handle under his seat, and the whole thing slid backward. She squeaked in shock as he reached over and pulled her entire body over on top of him. She barely had time to position her legs on either side of his hips before he set her down.

That shouldn't have been graceful. She should've messed that up and got them all tangled, but she hadn't. She kind of wished someone had caught that on video. She wasn't very good at stuff like that unless it was rehearsed and she'd had lots of time to mentally prepare—

Ooooh, Grim rolled his hips against hers, and now

his eyes were the bright gold of the Reaper. And that smile…the devil lived in that smile.

Ash cupped his cheeks. "Good man, bad man." She lifted her chin and looked him right in his eerie eyes. "My man. My monster. Mine no matter what."

His wicked grin faltered.

Take that, Reaper. Eat those nice words and figure out you won't be able to chase me away.

Ash leaned forward and pressed her lips to his. The snarl in his throat was instant as he gripped the back of her neck and pulled her closer. Harsh, sexy kiss. He pushed his tongue into her mouth, his hands rough on her neck and waist.

Ash loved it. She rolled her hips against him, slid her arms around the back of his neck, and held him tight. Fire trailed up her skin where his fingertips searched under her sweater. She could feel the back of his knuckles now, pushing up, up, until he found the bottom of her bra. His hands on her skin felt like everything she'd been thirsty for. Her breath came in short pants as he pulled his hand back and shoved her jacket off her shoulders. She struggled out of it, not so graceful now, because they were in the front seat of the SUV and he was a very big man. But he didn't seem to mind. He shoved her sweater up the second she freed herself from her coat.

This was normally the part where she would've flinched away and covered her stomach, but Grim's reaction to her body made it impossible to be shy. He let off a long moan and leaned back as far as he could, staring with those hungry gold eyes. His hands went to her waist, and they were so strong there. "Fuck, woman. You have me." There was desperation in his voice, and she wanted to cry and laugh and sing and hug him all at once for making her feel so good. For the first time under a man's stare, she felt like a queen.

It made her braver with him. If tonight was all they had, she didn't want to wake up tomorrow and think of all the things she wished she'd been bold enough to do. She just wanted to do them. So she pulled at the hem of his T-shirt. He lifted his arms for her and moved to help her. As the shirt was pulled out of the way, she let off a hungry sigh. His chest was massive with a perfectly cut line right down the middle, diving down into his six-pack abs that flexed with every breath. She was staring. She knew she was, but she couldn't stop. The upper part of his torso was covered in tattoos, but the artwork was stunning. It didn't hide the scars this close up, and she could see his chest was covered in crisscross patterns. How many times had he been badly clawed to mar his skin like this?

"Is this why you got the tattoos?" she asked, tracing a raised scar.

He pulled her hand to his lips and kissed her open palm. "It's not fun to see my past etched into my skin every time I look in a mirror."

Her heart broke a little for him. Or maybe opened up a little more for him. She leaned forward and pressed her lips to the worst scar. And then another and another until his hand went gentle in her hair and he relaxed back against the seat.

Ash ran her palms down the uneven skin of his stony chest, down the hard mounds of his abs to his jeans. She popped the button and filled the car with the sound of a slow zipper. His dick was swollen and hard, pressing against the fabric of his pants to be released. Grim lifted slightly so she could shimmy his pants down his powerful thighs.

When Ash gripped his dick in her fist and pulled up slowly, Grim let off a long, low, sexy sound in his throat, and his legs tensed under her.

"Grip it tighter," he murmured in a deep, gravelly voice that lifted chills onto her skin.

She tightened her fist and stroked him faster, and he flexed with the pace she kept. She could imagine him coming if they kept going like this. She could see it in her mind—him yelling out and jets of cum covering his chest. She'd never been this turned on. She rocked her clit against him with the rhythm of her stroking his cock.

The desperation to watch him finish warred with the need for him to be inside her.

"Oh, fuck, it feels so good," Grim groaned, his hands gripping her thighs, then her hips. He reached around and unsnapped her bra and yanked the thing from her arms. His hand was massaging her breasts before she even fully realized the relief of being out of the clothing. Grim pulled her forward and there was his mouth, clamped on her breast, his tongue licking her nipple until she was moaning over and over.

The rattle of his growl vibrated right through her chest, and she couldn't keep a single thought in her head. She was lost, on some high like she'd never been on before. Nothing in the entire world existed but her and Grim and the fire he was conjuring in her body.

With a snarl, he sucked hard one last time on her breast and eased back just far enough to pop the button of her jeans. He shoved her feet onto the floorboard to straighten out her legs and shoved the stiff fabric down to her ankles, panties and all. Damn near giddy, she kicked out of the constraints and climbed right back up onto his hips. There wasn't much room to move in here, but they were making it work fine. His dick touched her sex just right, and she rolled her hips against his erection. She was so wet, she slid right up and down him, and now he was kissing her again. Kissing and biting and nipping and kissing.

Ash was ready, so she sat up a little on her knees, ignoring the dang seatbelt buckle digging into her skin. She reached between them and gripped his dick again, angling it straight up. And then she slid down him by a couple inches. She hadn't been with anyone in a long time and should be rusty at this, but being with Grim was natural, like breathing or walking. Ash tensed her legs and pulled off him, then slid back down farther.

Apparently done with the tease, Grim slid his hands up her thighs, gripped her hips, and slammed her down hard on his cock. He filled her all at once and she gasped out, "Oh my god." It shocked her at how big he was. She could feel him stretch her insides. He stayed just like that for a few seconds, buried to the hilt inside of her, resting right against her clit. And then he pulled her off a few inches and yanked her back down. Then again and again. Her nerve endings were firing like crazy, and her entire body was tingling with how good it felt.

"Please," she whispered. Please what? She didn't even know what she was begging for, but apparently Grim did because he started bucking into her faster, his arms encircling her as their hips crashed against each other.

She was loud. She didn't notice at first, but there was a second of clarity right as her orgasm built to blinding pleasure where she heard herself screaming his name and heard the snarl in his words as he demanded, "Louder! Come on, Ash. Tell me how much you love it."

He was warm and she was warm and the vent was warm, and was she on fire? Her skin was crawling, and there was so much pressure in her middle. Her moaning was only getting louder and everything was so bright and "Fuck! I'm going!" she uttered helplessly as she sank her teeth into his collarbone. She didn't know what she was doing, only that her body was breaking apart in the best way.

He froze, buried deep inside her, and his dick throbbed hard. And then her insides were hot, too, as they throbbed together, jerking with ecstasy. Her body tensed every time he slowly bucked into her.

She tasted iron. Iron. Copper. Smelled like pennies. Oh no.

Her eyes flew open, and she released his torn skin and gasped.

Grim looked cocky as can be in the dim porch light that illuminated them from behind. His chest was heaving with his labored breath, and he had a thin sheen of sweat along his shoulders. A trickle of crimson snaked its way down his left pec, right over his heart.

There was one good-sized space left where he didn't have a tattoo filled in yet, right on his collar bone, and what had she done? Given him another gosh-dang injury! A mark!

"I didn't mean to hurt you!" she rushed out. Why was she still having an orgasm? She didn't deserve the pleasure!

"Oh, that wasn't you that hurt me. That was your bear. You're a little monster yourself, aren't you? Listen to her." His grin grew bigger and more sinful.

Her throat was scratchy from the growl in it, and she swallowed hard. That didn't stop the noise. "Oh, toot!"

Grim looked scandalized. "What the fuck is a *tewt*?" he asked, putting a funny accent on the word. She would've laughed if she didn't hate herself right now.

"Well, I was trying not to cuss right when we were…you know…"

"Say fucking."

"When we were fucking," she whisper-screamed. "So I said 'toot' instead of 'shit.' You're bleeding really bad!" She reached for her purple sweater and pressed it against the bite, but he swatted it away. She growled louder and put it back.

"You're going to ruin your sweater, and it's fine. You really bit me, Good Girl."

"Why are you smiling like that?" she asked,

utterly frustrated.

Grim shrugged. "I dunno."

But he did because she could sense lies, and he hadn't even tried to hide the lie in his tone.

She sighed fast and heavy and patted the bite with the sweater, but she'd bitten him really bad. "It's going to scar, and that makes me no better than the people who hurt you. I have some money in savings. I can pay for a tattoo to camouflage it. I'm so sorry!"

All of her words tumbled out like she'd said one long word, but he seemed to understand her just fine because he said, "I'm not sorry."

Was she crying? She was so uncomfortable and tingly, and her body didn't make any sense so she pressed her fingertips to her closed eyes but they came back dry. "You're confusing me."

"Am I?"

"Yes! And I...I..." Everything was so hot. Like someone had started a bonfire under the SUV. "I'm...burning up," she punched out through her panting. "Feel my forehead. Do I have a fever? I think I need to...do something." She couldn't inhale a good breath. Felt like someone was standing on her chest while holding a mountain.

Now Grim looked concerned, but she didn't have time to make him feel better. She had to make herself feel better first. Her skin was crawling like there were ants all over her. She shoved open the door and poured out of there like a Jell-O casserole out of a mold. Ash hit the snowy ground on her hands and knees and the first snap of breaking bone was like a gunshot in the dark.

"Oh, nooooo," she murmured quietly as she realized the awful thing that was happening.

The bear was coming. The bear was coming, and Grim would never forget this as the climax of their love-making and everything was terrible. She'd never figured out how to reverse a Change, though, and she couldn't put her broken bones back together until the bear decided she could Change back to her human form, so she gritted out, "I'm sorry," right before she stopped fighting. But the stupid Change was happening too slowly, so she rolled over onto her back and stared apologetically at Grim as he got out of the SUV.

"Are you okay?" he asked.

"Your dick is really pretty," she whispered. *Hurry up and Change! This hurts.* "Oh," she croaked out, "can you tell me if my bear is blue?"

Grim was fighting a smile as he knelt beside her.

"Be careful. I'm very dangerous."

"I think I'll take my chances," he said, moving her hair out of her face. "Why would you be a blue bear?"

"Because that's the real reason I let the hair school dye it blue, so I could see if I turn into a blue bear. I thought that would be kind of cool..."

"Oh, lord," he said, laughing.

"I'm very serious right now. Oooouuuuuhhhh," she groaned, curling in on herself as her spine started reshaping. "Your dick did this to me."

Grim snorted, and then he was laughing way too loud and hurting her head. "This is all on you. Your bear is like a little wrecking ball. She bit me, and now she's performing the slowest Change in the history of shifters."

"Everything huuuurts," she said, gripping her stomach. "This is my punishment for hurting you. This is karma."

But Grim wasn't laughing anymore, and when she looked up at him, he looked white as a ghost. "Grim?"

"Ash, I think you should..." He buckled. Or imploded. She didn't understand what her eyes saw.

It made no sense to her brain. He was a tattooed, mohawked behemoth of a man, and then suddenly, he wasn't there anymore. There was no transition; he was just a lion.

The animal towered over her, and she froze. She was mid-Change so what could she do to defend herself? Nothing. Not a damn thing. She was dead. This was how she was going to die—butt naked in the snow. She was going to die before she found out if the blue hair dye worked. Before she got to eat Dad's famous turkey-shaped pan of pizza rolls for Thanksgiving dinner this month. Before she had kids or even had sex a second time with Grim, and that part seemed just mean that she was going to be snuffed out before more Grim-dick.

But when he looked down at her frozen body, he didn't look pissed. Instead, his eyes were bright green.

He curled his lips back from those long, razor-sharp teeth and arched his head toward the sky before he let off a low, steady roar. Then another and another.

Something was happening to her body. The bear was reacting to the bellowing calls of the lion. Ash broke faster, Changed faster. Her bones reshaped and her muscles stretched and, in a flurry of pain and a smattering of pops, her bear came to be. She laid on the ground panting, eyes closed tight as the roaring died off. It echoed a few times through the mountains, growing softer and farther away with each one. Grim had called her animal from her. How was that even possible? He wasn't her Alpha. She was still pledged to the Boarlanders, the Crew she'd grown up in.

But here was Grim, doing Alpha shit, like prying a bear from her to stop her pain.

The bite on his shoulder was still bleeding, and if she could blush in this body, she would. His entire hide was marked up with scars. He had a thick black mane, and his glowing eyes were steady on her. Every step he took toward her was pure power.

Okay, if he bit her, she deserved it because she'd bit him first. And…karma.

But when he pressed his face against the scruff of her neck, she didn't feel the piercing of his sharp canines. No. He ran his tongue along her fur a few times and then sauntered off toward the woods.

She stood and shook the final tingles of the

Change from her fur. One peek at her black paws, and she grumbled a little growl. The blue hadn't worked. She was still just a plain dark-furred grizzly. But bright side...Grim stopped up ahead and turned to look over his shoulder at her. *I'm waiting for you. Come on.*

Ash trotted after him, happy that he was a book she could read when he was an animal, too. He was the best story. She bolted the last few steps and gave him a playful swat on his rump. He didn't even hiss at her as he started stalking toward the woods again. His lion still felt like a dominant brawler, and his scarred-up body would probably be intimidating to anyone else, but not to Ash. She loved every single thing about him.

This was the fastest any 10:10 wish had ever come true.

She'd wished he would stay The Good, and look at his bright green eyes as he walked right beside her, completely calm, attention casting her way every few steps.

10:10 really worked! Next time she would wish for more Grim-dick.

FIFTEEN

Ash couldn't sleep.

Beside her, Grim slept soundly, breath heavy and steady. He didn't even twitch, probably because of how well she'd put him to sleep. They'd stayed in the woods for hours. It was one of those magical nights. The Reaper had never shown up. Only The Good. They'd played and hunted a little but hadn't been serious about it. Mostly they explored together. And when they got sleepy, they made their way back to the house and Changed in the front yard. She'd gotten cold, but Grim had scooped up her naked body like she weighed no more than a bouquet of daffodils. And then he walked her right inside, got ready for bed, and then tucked her up tight against him.

"Turn over," she'd said, and he had. She'd ran her fingernails up and down his back until his body relaxed and his breathing deepened. He was hugging a pillow, and she hugged him.

But even though the back scratches had relaxed her, too, she couldn't make herself sleep because then she would lose minutes with him.

He had booked a flight for tomorrow at 12:05 pm, and it scared her, the thought she might never see him again.

He was already so important to her existence.

He would leave tomorrow, and Juno and Remi would leave with their mates as soon as Rhett was done recording his album. Ash would be left here alone again, nursing a big empty hole in her heart. When people got left behind, they didn't just cease to exist. They still had lives and hours to fill during the day, jobs and struggles. They still had sadness and joy. They still lived day in and day out, missing whoever had left them.

She didn't want to go back to that.

Her eyes teared up, and she pressed her palm against his warm, strong back in the dark. She rubbed it in a gentle circle, just to remind herself that it wasn't time for loneliness yet. He was here.

"Come with me," Grim said. But his voice was deep and dark and sounded like a demon.

Ash froze as something heavy wafted through the air and settled onto her skin. It felt like darkness. Ash leaned up just enough to see his reflection in the dresser mirror across the room. All she could see was glowing gold eyes. The Reaper. He was awake.

"I know you're killing me," he said.

Ash snuggled her naked body right up against him and laid a soft kiss on his back. "I don't want you to go."

A soft rumble vibrated against her cheek. "You don't want Grim to go."

"No," she whispered. "I mean, I don't want to kill you. You're important."

His growl was constant now. Soft but constant.

"I love Grim," she murmured. "And that means all of him. You included. I think he needs you and The Good both. It just hurts him when he only has you. When there's no balance."

He swallowed audibly in the dark and a rough, calloused hand cupped hers, pressed it against his stomach.

"If you kill me, it's okay. I still want you to come."

"Reaper," she whispered thickly, squeezing her eyes closed against the tears that wanted to come out. A strong man should hear when he's doing right. "I love you."

Grim tensed, then his hand went limp against hers and fell back to the mattress. His breathing steadied out once more. When she looked back at his reflection, he was asleep again.

With a sigh, she relaxed back onto her pillow, but she didn't take her hand away. Grim was on a journey, and she had this instinct that things would change for him.

He was growing, and she was going to miss it.

She was going to miss the best chapters in his book.

SIXTEEN

A sick day. Nursing a broken heart counted as a sick day, right? Audrey had let her off the hook so easy, too.

Grim was really gone. He'd had to be the Reaper all morning to prepare for a flight out to Tarian Pride territory, but she couldn't Change again so soon. So she'd sat on the porch on this frosty morning she would never forget.

She cupped her mug of hot coffee in her hands and shrugged deeper into the blanket. He'd said goodbye a half an hour ago, kissed her lots, but she was still here, stuck in a way, as her bear waited for her lions to come back. She'd done this for weeks when Juno had gone, and the same happened when Remi left.

Ash was careful of the people she chose, but when she picked one, her heart picked them for always.

The sound of a truck engine rumbled through the woods, and she sat up straighter, listening. It wasn't the SUV engine, though. It was another familiar man coming to see her. Bash Kane. That was the sound of Dad's new Raptor. She was pretty sure he'd bought it so he could match Clinton. They'd been great friends for years. They fought like a couple of old sisters, but when push came to shove, they always had each other's backs.

Clinton had a white one, but Dad had gotten one in the same shade of gunmetal gray as the old Dodge sitting in front of her cabin. His favorite color was orange, but for rigs, he liked dark gray.

He came barreling through the clearing like a bat out of hell (she'd never figured out what that saying meant, but Mom said it a lot) like he always did. He did three donuts in his truck, the tires spewing dirt and snow, and then he pulled up to her house and skidded to a stop.

"I don't know why I waited so long to get me one

of these," Dad said as he hopped out of the jacked-up truck.

"Because they cost more than if you sold all your organs on the black market," she reminded him, still unable to move from her seat. It was like her butt cheeks were frozen right here until Grim returned.

Dad was a sight for sore eyes, another saying she didn't understand. Sore eyes sounded like a terrible thing. He was tall and built like a brick house, and his hair was black like her natural color. Mom had always said Ash was the spitting image of him, down to her eye color and everything. Except Dad had a great big black beard and looked like a mountain man, and Ash sure hoped she didn't look like a mountain man.

Never the quiet person, Dad stomped right on up her stairs and took a seat next to her so hard, for a second she thought the swing would give. She'd reinforced it with double chains, but Dad was a very robust man.

He had a plate in his hands with foil on top, but she could smell what he'd made her.

"I like presents, and your mom said you're just like me, so I always knew what could make you feel better," Dad murmured. His eyes were sad.

"I do love presents," she said, forcing a smile so he wouldn't worry.

She removed the foil from the plate, but there were only two pizza rolls left and a bunch of grease prints from the ones that were gone.

"I had a snacksident." Dad looked remorseful, but she knew him. He might say sorry, but that man couldn't resist this food. He'd done good to make it here with two left.

She gave him one and popped the other in her mouth. "He went away."

Dad leaned back and stretched his legs, rocking the swing. "Audrey told me you sounded hurt on the phone."

"Well Audrey shouldn't worry people." She looked out to the trees again, her bear ever-hopeful that Grim would be standing there one of these times.

"I asked around about him. Grim. You like him?"

She nodded.

"I mean you like him, like him?"

Another nod, and now she felt like crying.

"He's a monster."

Another nod. The heart wanted what it wanted.

That was one of the few sayings she actually understood now.

"I felt like I was a monster once," Dad said, swinging them gently.

"What changed?" she asked.

"Your momma found me. Why are you still here, Baby Bear?"

Ash bit her bottom lip to keep it from shaking. She really hated worrying Dad. He was a simple man and got upset when anyone he loved was hurting. "What do you mean?"

"I changed all the seats on Grim's flight, and you have one right beside him."

Ash jerked her attention to her dad. "What?"

"I keep trying to teach you to check your emails, but you never do. You and your sisters never listen about your emails. I've sent you six this morning. I found funny memes, and none of y'all even called me to tell me I'm funny."

"Dad, I have a ticket on his flight?"

Dad checked his watch. "You gotta couple hours to make that flight. Pack light so you don't have to check a bag. That's me telling you not to pack six pounds of that eye glitter you keep smearing all over your face. Pretty girl lookin' like a bug light. You tell Grim I have about a dozen sets of eyes on him, and I will fuck his whole life up if he hurts you."

Ash jumped up, the blanket falling to the porch. "Dad, are you serious?"

"I'm very serious. I will kill him."

"No, about the flight!"

"Well, now you have one hour and fifty-nine minutes to get there. I'm not sitting here waiting with you while your bear watches people leave again. Just go with him and call me every day. And check your email."

Ash leaned down and kissed him quick on the cheek.

And as she ran into the house to pack, she could still hear dad talking. "I'm getting really good at meme-ing. And I've learned to make gifs. Honestly, I'm ready for one of your sisters, or maybe all of you, to start poopin' out cubs for me to play with. But your momma said I shouldn't say it like that because you aren't actually poopin' out cubs. But I saw you being born, and it sure looked like she pooped you out. I'm hungry again, so I'm leavin'. Vyr was asking questions about you and Grim, but I didn't know anything, so I told him to eat a dick and ask you himself. Clinton says I need to stop using his comebacks when I don't know what they mean, but he nodded like he was proud when I told Vyr to eat a dick. Your momma had her face all scrunched up, though. I'm probably in trouble. Okay, Baby Bear, I'm gonna go feed my belly. Message me when you land. Via email so I know you saw my memes. I love you!"

"I love you too, Dad! So much! You are the best dad!"

"I know! See you soon."

And then the sound of Dad's engine roared through the house as she was tossing about six pounds of eye glitter into her make-up bag, and Dad was off again.

No more waiting around for her.

She was going to do exactly what the Reaper had asked of her and go with Grim. For better or worse, she was going to march straight into Tarian Pride territory beside her man.

Bye, bye, boring life.

Helloooo terrifying, uncertain, questionable, adventuresome one.

SEVENTEEN

Grim sat in the back of the plane, looking at all the empty seats around him suspiciously. The attendant had announced it was a full flight, yet here he was, the only one sitting in the last two rows.

Fucking good! I don't want to sit by these stupid humans anyway. The Reaper was nice and agitated, probably thanks to being shoved in a plane and having a three hour flight ahead of him. He smiled at the flight attendant. "Can I get some vodka?"

"Ooooh," she said, her eyes going round. "We aren't supposed to serve the back alcohol until we take off. But you look like a shifter. Am I right?"

He inhaled deeply and muttered, "Yep."

"And the flight will probably go a whole lot smoother if you get what you want, right?"

"Yep."

"Then I would call these extenuating circumstances," she said with a kind smile. Patting her bouffant silver-streaked hair, she marched into the refreshments station in the little room in the back and began humming that "I've got a lovely bunch of coconuts" song.

People were starting to turn around and stare. Probably because of all the growling. "What?" he snarled.

Two normies turned back around. Wise humans.

Everything will be okay, The Good said. Grim had renamed him just for Ash.

Shit, thinking of Ash made his stomach clench.

Fuck off, pansy, the Reaper said.

Eat me, The Good said.

Gladly.

"Everyone just shut up and get along for three goddamn hours," he snarled.

The animals inside his head shushed, but now the humans were looking a might less comfortable. At least they wouldn't talk to him during the flight.

There was a bright side to having two assholes arguing inside of him. People steered clear of psychopaths.

Ash had cried when he left her. Just the thought of her sweet face...

Something pulsed dark inside of him so he rested his forehead on the seat in front of him and closed his eyes.

"Pardon me, 'scuse me," a familiar voice said from near the front of the plane.

Grim frowned so hard his face hurt. Oh great, now he could hear the Reaper, The Good, and the pebble in his pocket telling him in Rhett's voice to stop being a pickle-dick and go back to Ash. And now Ash's soft, submissive voice was clear as a bell.

Just load me up. Give me all the voices.

Everything was awful.

"Oh my gosh, I'm so sorry. I didn't mean to bop you in the head." Aw, make-believe Ash. He was going to miss her. Maybe her voice in his head wasn't such a bad thing.

"Hiiiiiiiii," make-believe Ash said from right beside him.

Be cool, be cool, be cool. She isn't really here.

You're wrong, fuckface, the Rhett-pebble in his pocket said. He even had a name for the stupid thing now. Rebble. Rebble the Pebble. The Tarian Pride should've just killed him when they had the chance. Put him out of his misery. He wish he'd never met Rhett.

Rhett is awesome and has a bigger dick than you, Rebble said.

Maybe if he dunked the little rock in a plastic cup of vodka, it would drown.

"Are you okay?" A hand touched his shoulder, and Grim nearly jumped out of his skin.

Ash stood there, blue eyes wide, looking just as startled as him.

"You're really here," he murmured.

"Well, I don't really want you to go to your old Pride alone. And I don't really want to sit around Damon's Mountains being sad that you aren't around. So"—Ash shrugged—"I packed in five minutes, and I'm pretty sure I forgot panties and pajamas and also a hair brush, but here I am." Her mouth ticked up into a nervous smile. "If that's okay."

Relief flooded his veins like a tsunami. "Hell, yes, it's okay."

"Oh, good. I got nervous for a second." She put a hard-topped purple carryon suitcase in the bin above them and sat in the seat beside him. And then she wrapped her arms around his bicep and settled everything inside of him with just a touch. He blew out a steadying breath as she began to tell him how her dad got her the plane ticket.

And when the flight attendant peeked around the corner and held up two miniature bottles of vodka, he shook his head and declined. He didn't need it anymore.

Because as he listened to his sweet Ash Bear talk, he realized something big.

Right now, hers was the only voice he could hear.

EIGHTEEN

It was dark by the time Ash and Grim rented a car, ate dinner, and drove to Tarian Pride territory. She was nervous from the second he eased onto an old one-lane dirt road. A few No Trespassing signs later, and Grim pulled up to a security checkpoint.

The second the man in the little one-room station saw Grim, he began speaking fast into a walkie talkie. Well, there was no getting in and out of here unseen.

"It's okay," Grim murmured, sliding his hand over Ash's thigh. "Rose knows we're coming, she's all packed, and there's nothing wrong with us being here. This used to be my home."

"Where the Reaper was born," she reminded him

gently. She didn't trust a single lion here except his grandmother.

Ash sent another text to Juno. *Where are you?*

Juno's response was immediate. *Off the plane, in a rental, speeding to you. Five minutes out.*

Hell, yes, Ash had called Rogue Pride. That's what Crew's did. They leaned on each other. Grim hadn't learned that yet because he wasn't brought up like she had been, in Damon's Mountains where shifters depended on each other. But going in alone like this, into a powerful Pride without a plan B was a bad idea.

"Hey, Zeke," Grim murmured through his open window to the guard.

Zeke was a tall man, but much lankier than Grim. He kept ducking his gaze, and his voice was quiet when he murmured, "They'll be waiting for you inside."

"They?" Grim didn't sound happy.

"Things have changed a lot around here since you left. Rose is at the pavilion." Zeke hit a button on the desk, and the automatic gate swung open slowly. There was a soft humming noise and a current in the air that said one touch of that metal fencing and a person would get the shock of a lifetime.

"Why do they need security?" she whispered. There were glowing eyes in the woods, reflecting in the headlights at every turn they made.

"They have a lot of enemies," he murmured darkly.

His body was strung tight like a bow string, and he sat rigid behind the wheel, gripping it so hard his knuckles were ghost white. "She was supposed to be at her house near the edge of the territory, not the pavilion," he snarled. Gold eyes. Grim had gold eyes now.

Ash tried to take a deep breath, but her lungs felt heavy and wouldn't work right.

Up ahead, there was a fork in the road, and Grim took the left one. A hundred more yards, and he pulled up to a pavilion that was open on three sides and had high rafters with exposed beams on the inside. There were picnic tables lined up and strands of outdoor lights hanging from the ceiling. A group of a dozen shifters or so were loosely gathered at the tables near the edge. And behind them sat a single female with long silky gray hair pulled back into a ponytail. She had high cheekbones, and though her face looked calm enough as she watched Grim pull to a stop in front of the pavilion, her body was every bit as tense as Grim's.

Something was wrong. She could feel it in her bones something was off. Something was coming. Something bad.

"Grim, I don't like this."

"Ash, you're safe. I won't let anything happen to you."

"Yes, but you are one lion, and they are…" She did a quick head count. "Twelve."

Grim chuckled and turned off the car. "You're right. It wouldn't be a fair fight. For them." Whoa, he sounded very confident.

Rose stood and made her way right through the males. Grim pulled his grandma against him as soon as she was close enough. As Ash got out of the car to meet everyone, she could barely make out his whispered words to his grandma.

"Are you okay?" he asked.

"There are things I haven't told you yet," she said, easing back and holding him at arm's length.

"You didn't answer my question," he growled, his attention jerking to the males who were moving closer.

Rose inhaled deeply and forced a smile for Ash, held out her hand for a shake. "I'm Rose. You must be Ashlynn."

Ash smiled shyly, stepped right up to her, and gave her a quick hug, ignoring her offered hand. "We hug where I'm from," Ash murmured. She cleared her throat and wrung her hands in front of her lap. "Grim said you were submissive, but you don't feel submissive at all."

"You sure do," a man piped up. "That surprises me, Grim."

"What of it, Todd?" Grim asked, glaring at him.

"Just a surprising choice in a mate is all. Seeing as how you're Tarian through and through and should know better." He spat. "She ain't even a lion, is she?"

"No," Grim said with zero hesitation. "Grizzly bear." He nodded his chin at Todd. "She might be quiet, but I'd bet on her fucking you up in a fight." He scanned the faces. "What is this?"

"An intervention," a tall man said from the shadows beside the pavilion. He stood from where he'd been sitting in a rocking chair and stalked closer.

Ash hadn't even noticed him there, and

apparently Grim didn't either because when he saw the heavily tattooed predator, his poker face faltered. "Ronin?"

"The one and only. I must say," the blond-haired man said in a silky-smooth voice, "I'm a little surprised you remember me."

"It's been a long time," Grim said, guiding Rose to stand on his other side.

The man, Ronin, reeked of dominance, almost as much as Grim, but was thinner and lither. He moved as if he concealed power. Just like Grim.

He didn't slow until he was right in front of Grim, and the two titans sized each other up. The tension was so thick it was hard for Ash to breathe. But suddenly, Ronin cracked a smile and pulled Grim against his chest. Grim clapped him on the back hard and laughed. "Oh man, it's been years."

"Too many years, old friend," Ronin murmured, releasing him.

"What the hell are you doing here? I thought you were clear of this place for good."

One of the men behind Ronin snarled, but Grim put him in his place immediately. "Aw, fuck off, Terrence. I can say what I want. You have a problem, we can take it to the clearing." Grim stared him down, fury radiating from him until Terrence dropped his gaze and exposed his neck.

"He doesn't mean any harm," Ronin rumbled. "Just loyal to me."

"Yeah, well, every one of them was once loyal to Justin, too. They turn easy." Grim gave Terrence an empty smile. "I learned that the hard way."

"Ronin," he introduced himself, offering a hand to Ash. His blue eyes were dancing as he pulled her hand to his lips and kissed her knuckles.

When Grim snarled out a single word "mine," Ronin released her. Smart man because Ash was about three seconds away from swiping her claws across his face. She didn't like uninvited touch that wasn't from Grim.

"Where is everyone?" Grim asked.

The spark left Ronin's eyes. "Council's dead and so is Justin. Killed by Dark Kane's Crew."

"I heard. Idiot went after Beast."

"Yep. The lions are trying to rebuild the council, and they started recruiting Tarian Pride members to make it up. They've split the pride right down the middle. Some want the council to be rebuilt, the ones looking for power, and some of us," he said, gesturing to the shifters behind him, "want a different future for lions. One without the rule of the council."

"Rebuilding the council with Tarian Pride members is the worst fuckin' idea in the world," Grim muttered. "Offense intended," he said to the milling group in the pavilion. "Lions here aren't known for their fair politics."

"Agreed," Ronin rumbled. "I came in to shake things up a little bit, but I can't do it alone. I'm in the middle of a war. Half of Tarian is in town, half are here. The townies have an Alpha they want on the throne." Ronin twitched his chin at the dozen men behind him. "But they seem to think I can turn things around for this Pride."

"Who do they have in town?"

Ronin shook his head. "New blood. Like me. Typical Tarian Alpha. Reminds me of Justin."

"Shhhit," Grim murmured. "You put another Justin on the throne, the Pride is doomed."

"Agreed."

Grim looked at Ash and Rose, then frowned. "Why did you bring me to the pavilion, Ronin?"

"I need an enforcer—"

"Fuuuck that," Grim snarled, walking back to the truck and pacing back. "Fuck that, Ronin. I'm not an enforcer anymore."

"What are you then? You aren't normal, Grim. You still have that damn monster in you. You're still the Reaper."

"No," Ash murmured.

"Just listen to him," Rose whispered.

"I know you hate what you are," Ronin said, "but this is you. No one can enforce like you can. No one could best you as Second. Together, we could change the entire infrastructure of our fucked-up shifter race. Me and you. Ronin and the Reaper."

"No," Ash repeated louder. "He's not just the Reaper. Not a weapon. He's The Good, too. He's Grim." *My Grim.* She couldn't lift her gaze from the stupid ground. "He can be happy. He's Alpha of Rogue Pride."

The scratching sound said Ronin was rubbing his beard in agitation, but she didn't care.

"My mate's right," Grim said.

Ash gasped and held his hand fast. "You said the M-word," she rushed out on a breath.

Grim murmured immediately, "Well you bit me,

woman."

"I know, but I didn't think you thought...I mean...I didn't know if you wanted..."

Grim lifted her hand to his lips and pressed a kiss against her knuckles, and all the chaotic jumbled mess of words in her head quieted. It was okay. He was okay, so she was okay. They could talk about this later.

Grim squeezed her hand and lowered it back down to his side. "I just came here to get my grandma out—"

"I don't want to go," Rose said softly.

"What?" Grim asked. "Then why did you tell me to come get you?"

"Because I wanted you to talk to Ronin face-to-face. You were such good friends as boys. Ronin was always a good boy, always had a good moral compass. It's part of why he couldn't stay in the Pride. And when the council saw how close you two were, even after they'd made the Reaper, they didn't want him messing with your moral compass."

"What moral compass?" Grim growled.

"Exactly," said Rose.

Ash had never seen anyone look so sad as Rose

when she murmured, "You didn't have a shot at changing your fate in this Pride, Grim. But Ronin was banished and raised well, and he can fix us. I know he can."

"At my expense?" Grim uttered softly.

"Your mate can stay here with us," Ronin said. "She'll have the protection of the Tarian Pride—"

"No," Grim murmured.

Ash held his hand tight because his eyes were glowing brighter.

"You can have a dozen cubs, lion or bear, won't matter. I just need you to—"

"No," Grim said in a sterner tone.

"Just back me up and be my Second, and when we go after the new council, you'll—"

"Kill?" Grim snarled. "Is that what you need from me, Ronin? Can you not feel him? Do you not remember what it was like for me when the Reaper was born? It got worse for me with every kill. Every drop of blood marred my soul and fed the devil inside of me. I left here wanting it all to end, and I found something I never thought could exist for a man like me instead."

Ronin looked pissed, and his breathing was

heavier as he stared down his nose at Grim. "And what's that?" he asked, the words tapering into a smile.

Grim tipped his head toward Ash. "Hope. And I'm pretty damn determined to keep it. I'm not your Second, Ronin. I'm Alpha of my own Crew of fuck-ups now. I'm keeping them."

"If the council is reinstated and Tarian Pride stays in the hands of the townies, who do you think they'll come for? When all the dust settles, who do you think they'll want to serve them?"

Grim made a clicking sound behind his teeth and gave Ronin his back. He pulled Ash toward the car.

"Don't walk away from me!" Ronin roared suddenly. "Who, Grim? Who do you think they'll come for? Your precious Crew of fuck-ups. They'll cut you off at the knees and starve you out. They'll take everything from you just like they did to me because that's what they do. If they want something, they take it, and they'll get you back. And in two years, you'll be standing right here remembering the chance I gave you to change everything!" Ronin strode toward them and yelled, "Reaper!"

And that was enough. A rattling growl in her

throat, Ash spun on him just as Grim did the same. He had his hand in front of her hip protectively as the lions surged forward, but whatever Ronin saw in her face made him stop in his tracks. Fury boiled through her blood, but her voice didn't shake when she said what she needed him to hear. To really hear and accept, because Ronin might have been a childhood friend of her mate, but he clearly didn't know the man he was now.

He wasn't anyone's weapon.

"His name is Grim, and his Reaper don't belong to no one but him."

As the last word left her lips, something terrible happened. Behind her came a monstrous roar that shook the earth. Heat blasted against her back, and she knew with certainty what she would find when she turned around.

A dragon was blasting fire in a line across the mountains. Grim had been right. He'd been right not to trust Vyr because something was wrong. He had mountains to take care of already. Why would he be setting fire to these? Terrified, she clutched onto Grim's hand and held tight.

"The Red Dragon," Rose murmured in a

frightened voice, eyes full of horror as the profile of the fire breather reflected in her terrified eyes. The snowy woods were glowing with fire. "What's happening?"

Grim looked sick as he watched the monstrous creature dive and eat more ash. "He's claiming these mountains." He looked back at Ronin. "The council and Alpha war are the least of your worries now."

NINETEEN

"I can stop him," Ash murmured, her heart pounding against her sternum.

"What?" Grim asked.

"I can stop him," she said louder. "Are they worth it? The Tarian Pride. Ronin. Are they worth letting them govern their mountains?"

Grim looked from her to Ronin and back. His eyes were the color of the sun as his mouth formed the answer. "Yes."

Adrenaline dumping into her system, Ash bent her head and texted Juno as fast as her flying fingers could type. *Vyr is burning the mountains. Can you see him? We have to stop him!* Send.

Head spinning, she kicked out of her shoes and stripped out of her clothes, then bolted for the woods. "Vyr knows me! I can fix this!" she yelled over her shoulder just as she hit the tree line.

It wasn't just protecting the Tarian Pride from whatever revenge Vyr had planned. It was keeping Vyr accountable for his dragon. Because once upon a time, Vyr had been a part of Damon's Mountains. He'd grown up with her, and she knew in her heart he was still good. But she also knew in her heart that if he didn't quit claiming mountains, he would get addicted to the power and lose himself completely. It wasn't the other dragons that the world should've been fearing all along. It wasn't Dark Kane, Rowan, or Harper. It wasn't Damon Daye, the ancient dragon himself. It was his son, Vyr.

She ducked a big branch and pushed her legs harder. This body was too slow, so she rushed her Change in desperation. She closed her eyes and pitched forward, landed on all clawed fours and kept running. Good bear, she was right there when Ash needed her. The grizzly was lightning fast when she wanted to be. *Please, let this work.*

Her breath chugged like steam in front of her face

as she raced for the dragon. Her claws dug in the snowy earth and her muscles stretched and warmed with her long strides. Faster and faster she went. She heard him before she saw him. Felt him on her heels—the Reaper. She wasn't scared. He wasn't chasing her. She cast a glance to her left, and he was there. Racing in the glow of the fires right along with her. His body was pure grace and power and hunter. Of course, he wouldn't leave her to do this alone. It wasn't in him.

Up ahead, she could see the crackling of flames licking at the trees. She could hear the roars of animals, but they were hard to identify over the noise of her own growling and breathing. Movement caught her attention, and on her other side were the lions. They were barreling toward the blaze right along with her.

And then there was the drumming of fists against a rock-solid chest. When she heard the challenge of a silverback gorilla, it changed everything.

Oh, no, oh, no! Torren, the son of Kong, was here. Which meant Nox, the son of the Cursed Bear, was here, too. Vyr's Crew was here to back him up.

Her biggest fear was realized as she and Grim

burst into a clearing fringed with dragon's fire. Torren's massive silverback gorilla and Nox's blond grizzly were charging two brown she-grizzlies. Juno and Remi were here, looking pissed as they aimed straight for Vyr's Crew. The Sons of Beasts were at war with the Daughters of Beasts, and nothing was okay.

Fucking Vyr.

Two enormous lions charged from the woods just as Juno and Remi clashed with Nox and Torren. Rogue Pride Crew had followed through and come right after them to have Grim's back just in case things went south with the Tarian Pride. Good Crew, but none of that mattered if they all died together tonight.

The sons and daughters of Damon's Mountains were at war.

This would echo through the mountains she'd called home for always.

Her heart was in her chest as she torpedoed with Grim toward the Red Dragon, who was circling for another pass. Ash couldn't tell if the white falling from the sky was snow or ashes.

All she knew was she had to appeal to Vyr's heart

before he burned a line in the earth, or he would be too far away for her to get into position again. She blasted right between Juno and Remi, then she looked back over her shoulder just in time to see Grim leap through the air and hit Nox like a cannonball. He freed up Remi, who bolted after Ash. Okay, good. Remi had guessed the plan then. Vyr was only going to pay attention to people he cared about. To people from Damon's Mountains, who he considered friends to protect. The lions, he would burn to ashes and eat them without a second thought. But Ash, Juno, and Remi? They stood a chance at surviving him. She hoped.

Weaving in and out of trees, Ash kept her attention on the uneven ground in front of her and on the sky where Vyr was diving toward them. He had lined up and opened his massive jaw, exposing a row of razor-sharp teeth. Shit, they were too far off. *Run, Remi!*

Ash pushed her body until her muscles screamed. Until her legs were blurring under her and she risked falling hard, but she couldn't slow down. She could hear Juno now, breathing heavy at her flank. All three of them were running as fast as they could, desperate to stop what was happening. To stop Vyr. To save him and save these people here.

Vyr's Firestarter clicked and echoed through the mountains. Time slowed to a crawl as lava and fire spewed from his mouth across the ground, aiming right for Ash and the girls. The wind from Vyr's wings was like a hurricane, and as she roared loud enough for the dragon to hear her, she uttered one name in her mind. *Reaper!*

The wall of fire came straight for her, Juno, and Remi. They were roaring, too, but the blistering heat was still coming. She saw the dragon's eyes just as he realized they were there. He clamped his mouth closed and beat his powerful wings, aiming for the sky, rumbling the earth with the sheer power of him changing directions, but it was too late. The fire had already left his mouth, and he hadn't pulled up in time.

Terror seized her in the last moments of her life, but just as she closed her eyes against the burning pain, something hit her like a battering ram from the back, and she pitched forward into a tree. Knives. That's what pierced her thick hide...right? Something was wrapped around her, stabbing her, blocking her from the sky. She knew his smell. With every breath she took in this life, she would recognize it. Grim had wrapped his body around hers and had his claws sunk into her, holding on as a wave of heat rippled against her cheeks. His body twitched, and he grunted in pain.

Stunned, Ash looked up to find Juno and Remi on the ground out of the way of the fire. Kamp and Rhett had knocked them clear into the woods.

It was the silverback charging through the dying flames that got her moving. Grim lurched up with her, and they ran for Torren. His massive fists punched the ground as he came for them, long canines exposed as he roared at Ash.

But something stopped Torren in his tracks, and he skidded through smoking ashes. He looked to the sky, nearly knocking into Ash. She looked up in time to see a blue dragon torpedo through the sky and slam into the Red Dragon.

Holy shit, Damon Daye was latched onto his son. They were both beating their wings, lifting higher and higher until they disappeared into the clouds. Bursts of flames spewed from the mouths of the beasts, illuminating the clouds and exposing their silhouettes as they warred.

Ash leaned heavily against Grim's golden-eyed lion as they watched the battle in the sky. She didn't know whether to be relieved or heartbroken that father and son were burning each other.

Up in the clouds, the fire stopped and the tips of their dragon wings sank down low enough to show through the clouds. They were flying east.

The clearing went still, other than the few burning blazes from Vyr. Dragon's fire burned hot and snuffed out quick so they could eat the ashes without consuming the flames, but there were places here and there that still burned.

Torren looked like hell. He was battered and clawed, and when he took a few hesitant steps toward her, heartache in his bright green eyes, Grim charged and let off a challenging roar. His back was burned from protecting her, but he didn't favor it. Tough mate.

Torren slammed his fists on the ground and said in a snarling voice, "I'm sorry."

Grim slowed to a trot and watched him turn around and leave with Nox's blond grizzly. They disappeared into the smoky woods, but still Grim stood sentry for her. His body was wrecked, but he stood straight with a proud lilt to his head, and when he let off a trio of short roars, Kamp and Rhett answered.

The Tarian Pride was across the clearing, loosely grouped and watching Grim.

He roared over and over, his frame tensing with the effort of each one until Ash couldn't help it—her bear had to answer back.

Why? Because Grim was bonding them. Not just her, but the entire Crew. How did she know? Because Remi and Juno were answering his call, too.

Ash stood proudly and watched her mate take his place at the head of Rogue Pride.

His Crew had shown up, and the Reaper had done something he'd never done before. He cared enough to claim them.

Ash hadn't killed him like the Reaper had predicted, and thank goodness for that. Instead, she'd softened him just enough to let people in. Good people. He'd compromised with The Good enough to give Grim balance. She could feel it now. She could sense it.

Grim would always hold more power than one

man should, but he wasn't so sick anymore.

His future wasn't impossible. His journey wasn't at the end of a road; it was at the beginning.

She'd always thought of Grim as this great book…

And now she could feel things turning around for him.

She knew it with such certainty…

His best chapter was starting now.

TWENTY

Ash was having a moment. It was an old, familiar feeling of uncertainty as she looked at her reflection in the hotel bathroom mirror. Where did she go from here? Where was home?

While her bear had laid it all out there for Grim and bitten him, her skin was still unmarred by a claiming mark. And perhaps it would always be like that. The mission to extract Rose was over. Ash didn't know if it was a failure or not, but Grim's grandmother had decided to stay with the Tarian Pride and even seemed happy about that decision at the dinner they'd had together last night.

So now what?

"You look so pretty," Grim murmured from the doorway behind her. He'd been sleeping on account of all the healing he needed to do. His back had been burned protecting her, but he acted like it didn't hurt at all. Maybe he was just used to aching. His eyes were hollow and he looked exhausted, but that smile... It was genuine and easy and made her chest flutter.

She shuffled over to him and leaned into his open arms where he held her for a long time. There weren't any words needed right now. The shock of the war still clung to them like a second skin.

She didn't know what would happen between Vyr and Damon or between the Sons of Beasts and Rogue Pride. She couldn't guess the future of the Tarian Pride. She didn't even know where to call home. She was only certain of one thing—she really loved Grim.

"I don't want to be apart," she said suddenly.

"What?" Grim eased back and cupped her cheeks. "Why would we be apart?"

A loud banging at the door sounded, and Rhett yelled through the barrier, "I got us all food. This probably isn't me kissing your ass because I want to be you Second."

"Give us a second," Grim called. "Ash, I don't want to be apart either."

Rhett called, "It's just you gave a specific amount of time, and it's been one second."

"I'm going to kill him," Grim murmured.

Giggling, Ash ran her hands down the curves of his strong shoulders. The man carried the weight of the world so well. "You won't kill him because deep down you care about him. And Kamp, Remi, and Juno."

"And?"

Confused, she asked, "And what?"

"And you. I care about you. More than anything. I would've never claimed this Crew if you didn't come along and make me feel salvageable. You made me feel worth a damn, despite all of my faults, and there are many of those. No one could've turned my head around like you. No one could've got me living again, but you."

Ash's lip trembled, and she dropped her gaze to hide the stupid weak tears building in her eyes. "I never thought someone would see me that way," she said in a very small voice.

"I do. You picked me when I wasn't worth a single

second of your time. You got devoted, you got tough, and you had my back from the moment I saw you. You are loyal, sweet, and submissive, but you aren't weak. You're the strongest woman I've ever met. You have a place with me, Ash. And, hell, it won't be easy. I'm no walk in the park, and I've never done this before. I feel like I'm going into this blind and with no tools. I know I'm gonna fuck up a thousand times before I start feeling like I'm getting the hang of taking care of you. But I want to learn. For you. For me. Because you changed the course of my entire life. You did that, Ash. You have that power." He chuckled and shook his head. "I'm an Alpha because of you, and I'm not even scared of failing them because I know you. You're a stubborn woman with her heart in the right place, and you won't let me fail. You're gonna make me work hard until I'm less shitty at this."

"It's been a minute," Rhett said. "I counted to sixty. I got you extra onions on your burger because you are a monster, and monsters like extra raw onions."

"I hate onions," Grim growled over his shoulder.

"Okay, I'm picking them off. This is the kind of treatment you'll get with me as your Second. Kamp doesn't even love you. He would never even get you food— Ow! Seriously, Kamp? You threw a boot at me?"

"Pretty sure I'm going to kill them both."

"I'll stop you," she promised.

"Mmmm," he said, the sound rumbling in his throat. "Vyr is off his rocker, but he said something the other day that stuck. He said to take care of my people until they cared enough about me to stop me if I go off the rails. You would do that, wouldn't you?"

"Yes," she whispered without hesitation. That was part of keeping him safe. He deserved protection, even if someday it was against himself.

"I would stop you, too," Remi called. "I would also be a good Second."

"Oh, dear lord." Grim rolled his eyes closed and sighed. He pulled Ash forward and pressed his lips against her forehead, then he leaned right against her ear and whispered, "I'm going to make a good Crew for you. If you'll have me."

"Have you how?" she asked, hope blossoming in her chest.

"If you'll be my mate."

She couldn't contain herself. She threw her arms

around his neck, stood on her tiptoes, and hugged him as tight as she could. And now she was making polka dots on his skin with her tears. "I never thought that was going to be my story," she said thickly.

"Me either. I think we just had to wait until we found each other. And we just...fit."

"You're the only person I've ever been able to understand. I thought I would be confused and lonely my whole life, but you fixed it."

"Shhhh," he said, rocking her gently.

"We're coming in!" Remi called.

The door opened with an awful creaking noise, and then her best friends and their mates lumbered through the hotel room door right to the bathroom and piled in. Rhett was holding a pile of onions in his hand and Kamp was missing a shoe. Remi was listing all the reasons a female should be Second in this Crew, and Juno was complaining about having something in her eye and poking said eyeball in the bathroom mirror. Grim let off a snarl so loud everyone stopped talking. It was gloriously silent for three seconds before he said, "I agree a female should be Second—"

"Yes," Juno and Remi hissed at the same time as

Kamp and Rhett groaned, "Noooo."

"And by that I mean Ash. Ash will be my Second."

"Oh, not me," Ash murmured, her cheeks heating. "I'm not dominant or even very smart about decisions."

Rhett snorted. "I'll say. You picked Grim— heeeyeeck!"

Grim's giant tattooed hand was suddenly around Rhett's throat, and he was glaring at him with bright gold eyes.

"Ash is a good choice for Second," Rhett rasped out.

Grim gave him an empty smile and released him.

"Okay, I agree with this decision," Remi said. "Ash will be a great Second. She's thoughtful and sweet, and any time Grim needs to calm down, she can just give him a blow job."

Grim pointed to Remi and deemed her, "Third." He pointed to Juno. "Fourth." Kamp. "Fifth." Rhett. "Last."

Rhett frowned deeply. "You could've said sixth, not *last*. But it's fine. You still picked me. I've brought you something to mark the occasion I became your first best friend but sixth Crewmate." He shoved his not onion-riddled hand deep into his pocket and brought out two mismatched paperclips. "I found them on the ground at the gas station."

"I don't want your trash, Rhett," Grim growled, pulling Ash by the hand toward the door.

"Why not?" Rhett called from behind them, following with the rest of the Crew outside and toward a pair of picnic tables across the parking lot. "It's like a friendship bracelet."

"I already have your stupid talking pebble in my pocket, Rhett. It's enough!"

As the boys groused at each other, Remi jogged up beside her and squeezed Ash's free hand and told her, "Welcome to the Crew, Ash."

The mushiest smile took over Ash's entire face.

And now Remi and Juno's eyes were all teared up, and Ash couldn't name another time she'd been so emotional or happy. Last night, everything had gone sideways, but today, none of that mattered. All that mattered was that she was here, right in the mix, not invisible or left behind. She'd been chosen by a good man who cared about trying and improving. She'd been chosen by someone she knew down to her bones would be a great Alpha. She was chosen by a man she loved right back. And now she would be in a Crew with Juno and Remi. How many childhood slumber parties had they spent dreaming about being in the same Crew someday? And look where she was now.

The best things were happening to her. To Ash. Oh, she knew it wouldn't be easy and their future was still uncertain. But she also knew they would be okay because she had her people—the people she'd chosen and become unerringly loyal to.

"Grim," she whispered, squeezing his hand.

"Yeah, Good Girl?" he asked, turning to her.

"Thank you."

The worry furrowing his dark eyebrows relaxed, and his face softened. "For what?"

She blinked back tears as she took in the organized chaos around them. The others were chattering on, settling on a picnic table, setting out food.

Thank you for the Crew, for believing in me, for giving me a home, for asking me to be your mate, for protecting me from the fire, for making me safe. There were a dozen thoughts at once, and as usual, her words got all mixed up. "For...for..."

Grim pulled her closer and leaned down, pressed his lips against hers. And then he said three words that filled her heart with joy. "I understand you."

Love meant something different to everyone.

For some, it was freedom.

For some, it was pain.

For some, it was a distraction.

For some, happiness.

For some, it was home.

But for Ashlynn Kane, love had been utterly...unattainable.

Until now.

Want more of these characters?

The Daughters of Beasts series is a standalone series set in the Damon's Mountains Universe.
More of these characters can be found in the following series:

Saw Bears

Gray Back Bears

Fire Bears

Boarlander Bears

Harper's Mountains

Kane's Mountains

Red Havoc Panthers

Sons of Beasts

About the Author

T.S. Joyce is devoted to bringing hot shifter romances to readers. Hungry alpha males are her calling card, and the wilder the men, the more she'll make them pour their hearts out. She werebear swears there'll be no swooning heroines in her books. It takes tough-as-nails women to handle her shifters.

She lives in a tiny town, outside of a tiny city, and devotes her life to writing big stories. Foodie, wolf whisperer, ninja, thief of tiny bottles of awesome smelling hotel shampoo, nap connoisseur, movie fanatic, and zombie slayer, and most of this bio is true.

Bear Shifters? Check

Smoldering Alpha Hotness? Double Check

Sexy Scenes? Fasten up your girdles, ladies and gents, it's gonna to be a wild ride.

For more information on T. S. Joyce's work,
visit her website at
www.tsjoyce.com

Made in the USA
Middletown, DE
07 March 2019